Someone who thinks like us . . .

"Since we're the Eight Times Eight Club, we need a new member," Erica informed me.

"We've given the matter a lot of thought," Gretchen said, glancing at Julia.

"That's right," Julia said. "The person we invite into the club has to be an eighth-grader."

"Has to be really cool," Marcy added.

"Has to think like us," Susan said.

So what did all this have to do with me? I wondered.

"After much deliberation, we've decided our new member should be . . . *you!*" Julia announced.

The other girls applauded.

I stared at them in disbelief. "Me?"

"That's right," Julia said, smiling. "You're pretty cool."

"Besides," Carmen said, folding her arms across her chest. "We've seen you watching us."

My mouth dropped open. "Watching you? I haven't been watching you," I argued.

"Yes, you have," Julia insisted. "But it's OK. We don't mind."

"Yeah, you're one of us now," Susan said, patting me on the back.

Bantam Books in THE UNICORN CLUB series.
Ask your bookseller for the books you have missed.

THE UNICORN CLUB®

TOO COOL FOR THE UNICORNS

Written by
Alice Nicole Johansson

Created by
FRANCINE PASCAL

BANTAM BOOKS
NEW YORK • TORONTO • LONDON • SYDNEY • AUCKLAND

To Gregory Wolf

RL 4, 008-012

TOO COOL FOR THE UNICORNS
A Bantam Book / January 1997

*Sweet Valley High® and The Unicorn Club®
are registered trademarks of Francine Pascal.*

Conceived by Francine Pascal.

*Produced by Daniel Weiss Associates, Inc.
33 West 17th Street
New York, NY 10011.*

Cover art by James Mathewuse.

ISBN: 0-553-48401-X
Published simultaneously in the United States and Canada

*Bantam Books are published by Bantam Books, a division of Bantam
Doubleday Dell Publishing Group, Inc. Its trademark, consisting of the
words "Bantam Books" and the portrayal of a rooster, is Registered in U.S.
Patent and Trademark Office and in other countries. Marca Registrada.
Bantam Books, 1540 Broadway, New York, New York 10036.*

PRINTED IN THE UNITED STATES OF AMERICA

OPM   0 9 8 7 6 5 4 3 2 1

One

OK, I'll admit it. I was in a bad mood. Maybe that's why the Unicorns were getting on my nerves.

We were hanging out in Jessica Wakefield's family room, listening to her make prank phone calls, of all things. "All right, you guys," she said, her bluish green eyes twinkling mischievously. "It's ringing."

Mandy Miller and Ellen Riteman crowded in beside her. "Shhh!" Ellen giggled and Mandy put her finger to her lips.

Jessica cleared her throat as she tossed her long blond hair over her shoulder. "Hello," she said in her most grown-up-sounding voice. "I'm calling from the National Refrigerator Association. I need to know, is your refrigerator running right now?"

I raised my eyebrow. *The National Refrigerator Association?*

Ellen snorted loudly. Mandy cuffed her on the arm as she chomped on her grape bubble gum.

I yawned and turned to Lila Fowler, who was carefully painting her fingernails purple.

In case you're wondering why purple, it's our club color. We picked it because it's the color of royalty.

When I think of royalty, I think of kings and queens. Fancy balls. Beautiful dresses. Elegance. *Not* prank phone calls.

"Well, then you better go catch it!" Jessica shrieked. She slammed down the receiver. Ellen, Mandy, and Jessica all collapsed in a fit of giggles.

Lila blew on her wet nails. "You guys are *so* bad!" She laughed.

Immature was more the word I had in mind.

Maybe it was just me. I'm fourteen and in the eighth grade at Sweet Valley Middle School. All the other Unicorns are in seventh grade. It could be you start to see things a little differently when you're in eighth.

I mean, eighth grade is practically high school. How many high-school students call people up and ask them if their refrigerator is running? Not many, I bet.

Ellen picked up the phone and handed it to Jessica. "Do another one," she begged.

"Oh, please don't," I said, rolling my eyes. I couldn't help it. I'd had enough.

Everyone stared at me in stunned silence.

"Don't you guys think this is just a little bit immature?" I asked, glancing at each one of them.

"Immature?" Mandy said as though she'd never heard the word before. She blew a huge purple bubble. "Who are you calling immature?" she asked.

Jessica planted a hand on her hip. "Yeah. Who died and made you Queen of Maturity, Kimberly?"

"Really!" Lila chimed in.

I sighed. You'd think that Lila, at least, would get my point. I mean, her dad's totally rich, so she's been able to go a lot of places and do a lot of things that the rest of us haven't. But apparently that kind of life hasn't taught her a thing about maturity.

Ellen bit her lip. "Come on, you guys. Let's not fight," she said softly. Her parents had just gotten divorced, so she was especially sensitive. But she was getting on my nerves as much as everyone else was.

Ellen can be such a baby. She even looks like a baby. She wears her brown hair cropped short with bangs in front. I don't think she's changed her hairstyle since she was in second grade.

But there was no reason to point that out. Like I said before, I was in a bad mood. And when I'm in a bad mood, it's usually best if I just keep my mouth shut.

My mood didn't improve any when Elizabeth the Saint Wakefield burst into the room. "Hey, you guys!" she said breathlessly. "Did you hear the news?"

Elizabeth is Jessica's identical twin sister. They have the same sun-streaked blond hair, the same blue-green eyes, even the same dimple in the left cheek. I'm telling you, if they had the same personality too, I'd find myself a new club. Elizabeth is *such* a goody-goody.

Jessica glanced up at her twin. "What news?"

I picked up Jessica's copy of *Teen Dream*, which was lying on the coffee table. I'm sure Elizabeth's idea of "news" was something along the lines of new uniforms for the chess club.

"Johnny Buck is playing at the Sweet Valley Amphitheater weekend after next!" Elizabeth announced.

I looked up.

"What?" Jessica and Mandy said in unison.

"Are you sure?" Ellen asked excitedly.

"That is so great!" Lila put in.

I almost got really pumped too. But being the oldest and most mature person in the room, I, of course, thought of the one thing that just didn't make sense here. "If Johnny Buck is playing in Sweet Valley in less than two weeks, why haven't we heard about it before now?" Even more to the point, why would *we* be hearing it from *Elizabeth?*

I'll say one thing about the Unicorns: We know just about anything worth knowing.

Elizabeth shrugged. "All I know is he was scheduled to be in Las Vegas that night, but the arena that booked him has some sort of electrical problem. They're going to be closed for a while. And there was no other place in Las Vegas that Johnny could move to. So he canceled that performance and decided to come here instead. Tickets go on sale at Great State Music first thing Saturday morning."

So it was true—Johnny Buck was coming to Sweet Valley. My bad mood suddenly evaporated. Poof! Just like that.

"Oh! We have to go!" Ellen squealed, jumping up and down.

"Of course we'll go," Mandy agreed.

"We'll get up really early Saturday morning," I said. "So we can be first in line for those tickets."

"Yeah, like five A.M. or something." Jessica nodded.

"Five A.M.?" Lila wrinkled her nose. "You mean like five A.M. in the morning?" She groaned. "How about we draw straws to decide which one of us has to get up and get tickets for everyone else."

Mandy tossed a throw pillow at her.

"No way!" I shook my head. I was really getting into the spirit of things now. Club unity and all that. "If one of us is going to camp out at five A.M., *all* of us are."

"Yeah, it'll be fun," Mandy said.

"We can bring doughnuts and hot chocolate," Jessica suggested.

"And magazines for something to do," Mandy added.

"I've got a magazine of word search puzzles," Ellen offered.

"Word-search puzzles?" Lila blinked with surprise.

I was glad she said it and not me. I didn't want to be the club grouch. But really! I hadn't done a word search puzzle since about fourth grade.

But Ellen only shrugged. "What's wrong with word search puzzles?" she mumbled.

"Hey, I've got an idea," Mandy said, cracking her gum. Suddenly the gum fell out of her mouth. "Oops." She giggled. "Sorry."

She picked up the purple wad from her jeans and popped it back into her mouth.

I cringed. Could she possibly be more disgusting?

"How about we get some T-shirts made that say 'I Love Johnny Buck,'" Mandy suggested. "We can wear them when we get the tickets and when we go to the concert."

"You mean you want to wear them *twice! Out in public?*" Lila had so many clothes that she never wore the exact same thing twice.

"I don't know." I grimaced. "Wouldn't we

look like a bunch of starstruck teenyboppers wearing shirts like that?"

"How about instead of shirts that say 'I Love Johnny Buck,' we get one shirt that says 'We' and another that says 'Love' and another that says 'Johnny'—" Suddenly Ellen stopped. "Oh," she said, sounding a little embarrassed. "There are *five* of us. 'We Love Johnny Buck' is only four words."

"That's OK!" I shuddered. "You guys wear them. I'm not into wearing *part* of a message on my chest."

"But you have to, Kimberly," Mandy said, putting on her lost-puppy look. "Otherwise it's not a true Unicorn thing."

"I know!" Jessica spoke up. "The fifth shirt could have an exclamation point. Kimberly, you could wear that if you don't want to wear one of the words."

I raised my eyebrow. I was *not* going to wear an exclamation point.

"Or instead of 'We Love Johnny Buck,' we could spell out 'We Love *You*, Johnny Buck,'" Ellen said, looking pretty pleased with herself. "That's five words."

"Oh, that's good!" Mandy nodded her approval.

"*Really* good!" Jessica agreed.

"I don't know." Lila hesitated. "Wouldn't that be sort of . . ."

Yes! Go ahead and say it, Lila. Immature!

"Weird?" Lila finished. "I mean, we'd have to walk around in order."

"So?" Mandy shrugged.

"It'll only be for a couple of hours at a time," Jessica pointed out.

That was about four hours too many. "Listen, you guys," I spoke up. "I have to agree with Lila here—"

"I'll do it if I can wear 'Johnny,'" Lila said suddenly.

Ellen giggled.

Mandy blew another bubble.

"All right," Jessica said. "It's settled, then."

Excuse me? Settled?

"Everyone's going to be looking at us," Jessica said with a grin.

I sighed. That was exactly what I was afraid of. To Jessica, attention was attention. She didn't seem to understand there was such a thing as *negative* attention.

"I'll have to call Janet as soon as I get home," Lila said as she and I walked home together from Jessica's house.

Janet Howell is Lila's cousin. She was president of the Unicorn Club last year before she went off to high school. "I know she'll want to go to the Johnny Buck concert."

"Do you think so?" I asked hopefully. I hadn't

seen Janet or any of the Unicorn Club graduates since I'd been back. Back from Atlanta, that is.

We moved clear across the country to Atlanta, Georgia, at the beginning of the year because of my dad's job. Atlanta was OK, but I really missed Sweet Valley. So I was glad when my dad's company moved him back here.

But it's like everything totally changed in the short time I was gone. I always knew Janet, Tamara Chase, and Grace Oliver would go off to high school. But I didn't know Belinda Layton would switch to private school. And I didn't know that I'd be the only eighth-grade Unicorn left.

When I first came back, Elizabeth Wakefield and her goody-goody friends were Unicorns! Can you believe that? Fortunately I put a stop to that right away. But still. Something about the Unicorns just hasn't been the same ever since.

"That would be so cool if we could all go to the concert together," I told Lila. "The five of us plus Janet, Tamara, and Grace. It would be just like old times."

Lila blinked. "Well, I think Janet will probably want to go with Cindy," she said matter-of-factly.

I frowned. "Who's Cindy?"

"Her best friend," she said, as though I should have known.

"Oh," I responded. I had forgotten Janet had a new best friend. Someone who'd never been a Unicorn and hadn't even gone to Sweet Valley

Middle School. "Well, I guess Cindy could come too." It would be good to meet the other kids that Janet, Tamara, and Grace hung out with. That way I'd see who my friends were going to be next year.

"Um, Kimberly," Lila said carefully. "Now that Janet's in high school, she sort of has her own friends. I mean, we still talk on the phone since we're cousins. But we don't hang out much."

"Oh," I said. So much for things being like old times. Come to think of it, after today's Unicorn Club meeting I could see why Janet wouldn't exactly want to spend much time with Lila or the other seventh-grade Unicorns. But I didn't tell Lila that. Sometimes I wished I could just go right on to high school and skip the rest of eighth grade.

"Oh, good, Kimberly. You're home! Hi, Lila," my dad said, bounding down the front steps. He had this really goofy grin on his face, like a little kid who had just learned a new trick. Then I saw the deck of cards in his hand. I groaned. Dad *had* learned a new trick.

This is really embarrassing, but my dad has taken up a new hobby. Magic.

At his last physical his doctor said he'd been working too hard. That he needed to find a hobby. Most people choose something like gardening or woodworking. But not my dad. No, my dad chooses magic.

"Hey, Mr. Haver. How's it going?" Lila asked politely.

"I'm glad you asked that, Lila," Dad said with a smile. "How would you like to be the first to witness my new magic trick?"

Lila looked at me uncertainly. "OK," she said, shrugging.

"Big mistake," I muttered. You see, my dad's not exactly *good* at his new hobby yet. So when he flubs up, he has to do it again. And again. And again. Until he gets it right. We could be here all night.

"Pick a card," Dad instructed Lila.

Lila chose one from the middle of the deck.

"OK, put it in your pocket," Dad said, shuffling the rest of the deck.

Lila glanced down at her green stirrup pants. "I, uh, don't have any pockets, Mr. Haver."

"No pockets?" Dad said with alarm. He scratched his head. "I can't do the trick without pockets."

"Too bad," I said, snapping my fingers. "I'll call you later, Lila." I was trying to do her a favor by giving her an escape. But Dad just wouldn't let her leave.

"You've got pockets on *your* jeans, Kimberly," he pointed out.

"Dad—" I started to protest.

"Kimberly!" Dad mimicked my tone of voice. "Come on, honey. Lila wants to see this trick before she goes."

Lila giggled. I think she was enjoying my embarrassment.

"Oh, all right," I said with a sigh. I grabbed the card from Lila. Three of diamonds. Then I stuffed it in my back pocket. "Now what are you going to do?" I asked Dad impatiently.

"I'm going to pull your card out of the deck," he said with confidence.

Yeah, right, I thought, folding my arms across my chest.

Dad shuffled through the deck. He pulled out the nine of clubs. "Is this your card?"

Lila bit her lip and glanced at me out of the corner of her eye. "No," she replied.

Dad frowned. He pulled out another card. "How about the queen of hearts?" he asked.

Lila giggled. "Sorry."

He tried one more. "Ten of spades?" he asked weakly.

By this time Lila was laughing so hard, she could barely shake her head no. I rolled my eyes.

"I think you better practice some more," I told Dad, giving him a gentle shove toward the house.

"All right, all right. I can take a hint," he said, turning and heading up the front walk.

"Better luck next time, Mr. Haver," Lila called to him.

Dad waved to her from the porch.

"Sorry about that," I said, once he was too far away to hear.

"Are you kidding?" Lila snorted. "I think it's cute that your dad wants to be a magician."

I couldn't help grinning. The Unicorns may be a little immature sometimes, but one thing I can say for them. They don't hold the goofy things your parents do against you.

Two

"I can't believe you're moving," Julia Abbott cried just before history class the next day. I mean, she was *really* crying. There were actual tears running down her cheeks. And everyone was looking at her.

"I know," Amanda Harmon responded. "I kept hoping it would turn out to be a horrible mistake. But it's not. The moving van is at my house right this minute."

Gretchen Weber sighed. Gretchen, Amanda, and Julia were all members of the Eight Times Eight Club, otherwise known as the Eights. The club is made up of eight eighth-grade girls. Amanda Harmon is their president.

I couldn't wait to tell the Unicorns that Amanda was moving. The Eights and the Unicorns have had this rivalry ever since they were pitted against each other on the TV show *Best Friends*. That was when I was still in Atlanta.

The Eights *creamed* the Unicorns. And then when the show was over, they made the Unicorns sing "Puff the Magic Dragon" during lunch. The two clubs have been archenemies ever since.

"So what's going to happen to the infamous Eight Times Eight Club when Amanda moves away?" Bruce Patman asked, running his hand through his wavy dark hair. Bruce can be obnoxious, but everyone thinks he's totally cute.

"I don't think we should be talking about that right now," Julia hissed, nodding respectfully toward Amanda.

But Bruce isn't the most sensitive guy in the world. "Why not?" he asked briskly. "She's just moving away. It's not like she's *dead*."

Amanda glared at Bruce, then turned back to Julia. "Bruce is right," she said with a sniff, obviously trying to be brave. "I expect the Eights to carry on without me." She paused as she glanced around the room. "Of course you'll need a new member. This is the Eight Times *Eight* Club, not the Eight Times *Seven* Club." It was like she was checking out every single girl in the class, considering who might be worthy of filling her shoes. "I trust you'll choose someone very cool," she said.

I wondered who they could possibly choose.

One thing about the Eights. They dressed the same. They wore their hair the same. Everything about them was the same. Who else would fit their mold?

Mandy says the Eights are total clones, all following Amanda's lead to the letter. Mandy hates conformity. But personally, I kind of liked the way the Eights do everything alike. They're like a college sorority or something. Sometimes I wished the Unicorns were more like that.

But maybe it's a good thing we're not. I mean, considering the way my friends have been acting lately, I wouldn't want to seem just like *them*.

"Psst! Kimberly," Julia hissed from across the aisle.

I turned. We were supposed to be answering questions on the causes of the Civil War, but hey! Anything for a distraction.

"Meet me in the bathroom by the office after class," she whispered.

I frowned. "What for?"

"You'll see," she whispered mysteriously. There was a little twinkle in her greenish eyes. Then she went back to her assignment.

Like I said before, the Unicorns and the Eights were not exactly friends, so I had visions of getting my head flushed down a toilet. Except it's almost always boys who do that.

Maybe she wanted to compare answers on the

history assignment? No, she'd probably do that with the Eights.

Or maybe she had a message from the Eights to the Unicorns? So why tell me? *Ellen* is our president.

Maybe she just wanted to borrow my lipstick?

Whatever it was, I was pretty curious.

"What do you think of our office, Kimberly?" Erica West asked, gesturing grandly around the bathroom.

All the Eights were there—Julia, Marcy, Carmen, Gretchen, Susan, Kristin, and Erica. Everyone except Amanda. They were all wearing black jeans with red blouses.

"Your *office?*" I asked, raising an eyebrow.

"Yup," Julia replied. "Our official headquarters at school."

"But don't tell anyone," Kristin said, putting a finger to her lips.

Headquarters at school? Why didn't the Unicorns think of that? We had the Unicorner, which was our official table in the cafeteria. But that wasn't the same thing. We couldn't just go hang out there between classes.

"We meet here because no one ever uses this bathroom," Julia informed me, fluffing her shoulder-length blond hair with her pick and watching me in the mirror.

"That's because it's so close to the principal's

office," Susan put in. She elbowed her way in between Julia and Erica and started fluffing her hair exactly like they were fluffing theirs. The three of them could have passed for sisters. They all had the same shoulder-length wavy blond hair.

"Need a pick?" Marcy asked, offering me hers.

I looked at it. "Uh, no," I said quietly. I fumbled with the zipper on my purse. "I've, uh, got a comb right in here."

I was still wondering why Julia had asked me to meet her here. Especially if this was their club headquarters. What did they want?

The Eights reached for their purses at the same time, as if some invisible signal had gone off. They put their picks away and snapped their purses closed. Then they formed a circle around me.

"I suppose you're wondering why we called you here," Julia said in a serious voice.

"Well, yeah," I said, glancing around the circle. "The thought had crossed my mind."

"As you know, Amanda Harmon is moving," Susan told me.

"To Sacramento," Kristin added.

"Today," Carmen put in. "Yesterday was her last day at school."

It was kind of cool how they each took part of a sentence. Like they knew exactly what the others were thinking.

"Since we're the Eight Times Eight Club,

we need a new member," Erica informed me.

"We've given the matter a lot of thought," Gretchen said, glancing at Julia.

"That's right," Julia said. "The person we invite into the club has to be an eighth-grader."

"Has to be really cool," Marcy added.

"Has to think like us," Susan said.

So what did all this have to do with me? I wondered.

"After much deliberation, we've decided our new member should be . . . *you!*" Julia announced.

The other girls applauded.

I stared at them in disbelief. "Me?" I would have been less stunned if they'd said they were all going to shave their heads.

"That's right," Julia said, smiling. "You're pretty cool."

"And you've had experience being in a club," Kristin pointed out. "So you know what to expect."

"Besides," Carmen said, folding her arms across her chest. "We've seen you watching us."

My mouth dropped open. "Watching you? I haven't been watching you," I argued.

"Yes, you have," Julia insisted. "But it's OK. We don't mind."

"Yeah, you're one of us now," Susan said, patting me on the back.

I pulled away. "Um, listen, you guys," I said hesitantly. "This is really nice of you and everything, but I've got my own club. I—I—I can't join yours."

A shadow passed over Marcy's face. "Sure, you can," she responded. "All you have to do is tell the Unicorns you'd rather be in our club now."

"Yeah, they'll understand," Carmen said.

I almost burst out laughing. *Sure, they would.*

"After all, you're an eighth-grader like us," Marcy said, shrugging.

"The Unicorns are all seventh-graders," Erica added with a knowing glance around the circle.

"You don't really want to hang out with a bunch of seventh-graders, do you?" Gretchen asked. She made it sound like the difference between seventh grade and eighth grade was about ten years.

"Yeah, what are you going to do next year when you go off to high school and they're still back here?" Carmen wanted to know.

"Well, there are former Unicorns at Sweet Valley High," I pointed out.

"Uh-huh." Kristin folded her arms across her chest. "And how often do you see them?"

"Face it, Kimberly," Carmen said grimly, "by the time *you* get to high school, they'll have forgotten all about you."

No! I thought. Janet and the others wouldn't forget about me.

"You won't have any friends," Susan added.

"Unless you join us." Julie smiled sweetly.

They were crowding in on me, pressing closer

and closer. I started backing toward the door.

"Look, I'm really sorry, you guys," I said, swallowing hard. "I'm totally flattered and everything, but I can't join your club. I just can't!" And then I ran out of the bathroom.

"Let's see them!" Ellen squealed with delight. The other Unicorns and I had just come from Expressly for You, where we'd had our stupid designer T-shirts made. Now we were clustered around a bench outside Casey's while Jessica opened her shopping bag and pulled out five purple T-shirts with white letters.

"Cool!" Mandy said with approval as she glanced over Jessica's shoulder.

Jessica passed the top shirt to Ellen. "We," she said with a grin. Then she passed the second one to Mandy. "Love." She passed the third to me. "You."

I rolled my eyes.

She kept the fourth shirt herself. "Johnny." And she gave the last to Lila. "Buck."

"Excuse me, Jessica," Lila objected as she yanked Jessica's shirt out of her hand. "But you said *I* could wear 'Johnny.'"

Jessica grabbed the shirt back. "What's the big deal?" She shrugged. "I gave you 'Buck.'"

"Yeah, and you kept 'Johnny' for yourself!" Lila raised her voice and reached for the shirt again. But Jessica yanked it out of Lila's reach.

"Careful," Mandy cautioned. "You guys are going to rip that shirt."

"But it's not fair!" Lila whined, stomping her foot. "Jessica said I could wear 'Johnny.' You all heard her."

"Why don't we just skip this whole thing," I said, handing my shirt back to Jessica. I still wasn't crazy about this T-shirt idea anyway. "I mean, if you guys can't even agree on who's going to wear what . . ."

"Oh, fine!" Jessica said huffily, throwing her shirt at Lila. "Take it if you're going to be such a baby."

Personally, I thought they were both acting like babies.

Jessica glanced down at the shirt I had thrown over her arm. "This is yours, Kimberly," she said, handing it to me.

I shook my head, refusing to accept it. "Just forget it. This is a stupid idea anyway." I sat down on the bench and crossed my legs.

Mandy sighed. "It doesn't matter which shirt any of us wears," she said diplomatically.

"Yeah. The important thing is we're showing our appreciation of Johnny Buck," Ellen put in.

Mandy pumped her fist in the air. "We love Johnny Buck!" she cried.

"We love Johnny Buck!" Ellen echoed.

Could they possibly be more embarrassing? "You guys?" I said with a heavy sigh. I glanced from side to side. "People are looking at us."

"We love Johnny Buck!" Jessica and Lila piped in. I almost wished they'd go back to their petty little argument.

"I don't even know you guys," I muttered, scooting down on the bench away from them. What were they thinking anyway? I mean, it was one thing to like Johnny Buck, but you just don't start chanting it in the *middle of the mall* like that.

Just when things couldn't get any worse, I noticed the Eights walking toward us in a line. Not that I cared so much what *they* thought, exactly. But I don't think I'd ever see them traipsing through the mall yelling out, "We love Johnny Buck!"

"Hello, Kimberly," seven voices said in unison. They stopped right in front of us and looked at us like we were third-graders.

I couldn't help but admire their silky red jackets with the black eight-ball patches on their sleeves. The Unicorns used to have jackets, but that was the beginning of the year when Elizabeth and her friends were Unicorns. I never had one of those. Which was fine. I certainly didn't want a jacket Elizabeth Wakefield or Maria Slater had worn. The very idea of it gave me the willies.

The Unicorns stopped chanting. They looked from me to the Eights.

"What? Are the rest of us invisible?" Mandy planted a hand on her hip and cracked her gum.

Kristin Benson snorted. She looked at Mandy like she was an insignificant speck of dust.

Marcy Becker shot me a look that said, "Poor Kimberly."

Julia Abbott glanced questioningly at the others. When Carmen and Susan nodded, Julia turned back to me. "We just want you to know, Kimberly, the offer still stands," she said, resting a sympathetic hand on my wrist.

Then they slowly strolled away.

Great, I thought.

The Unicorns watched the Eights with their arms folded across their chests.

"What was that about?" Jessica demanded, turning to me once the Eights were out of sight.

"Yeah, what *offer?*" Lila asked, frowning.

"Uh, Julia offered to let me study with her and some other people for this big history test we're having next week," I said quickly.

Jessica snorted. "Why?"

"Yeah. Why would you want to study with them?" Ellen asked suspiciously.

"I don't," I said quickly. "They were just, I don't know, being nice."

"One of the *Eights* was being nice?" Mandy asked, wide-eyed. "You've got to be kidding!"

Lila and Jessica laughed.

"Come on, you guys," Ellen said, grabbing

Mandy's arm. "Let's go get something to eat at Casey's. I'm starving!"

"Me too," I said, grateful for the distraction.

There was no reason the Unicorns needed to know I'd been invited to join the Eights. I certainly wasn't going to join, after all.

Three

"Kimberly? Hi, it's Julia Abbott."

My heart pounded as I held the phone to my ear. "Um, hi, Julia," I stammered.

Why was she calling me? Was she going to say something about how immature the Unicorns had acted at the mall earlier today?

"You're probably wondering why I'm calling," Julia said as if reading my mind. "You probably think I'm calling to hassle you about joining the Eights."

"Well—"

"Don't worry," Julia interrupted. "I'm just calling to see if you happened to copy down the history assignment."

"History assignment?" I repeated, a little confused. I mean, why ask *me* about the history assignment? Most of the Eights were in that class too.

"Um, just a minute," I said, reaching for my notebook. "We're supposed to read chapter twelve and answer the first five questions at the end."

"Thanks a lot, Kimberly," Julia said as though I'd saved her life or something. "You're a real friend."

"No problem."

"Oh, one more thing," Julia said. She let out a small laugh. "I gather the Unicorns are Johnny Buck fans."

I felt my face heat up. I should've known she'd bring up that embarrassing moment at the mall. "Uh, yeah . . . ," I said cautiously.

"So are we," Julia informed me. "Are you guys going to the concert?"

"Yeah," I responded. "We're going to camp out at Great State Music early Saturday morning."

"We've already got tickets," Julia said, sounding proud. "Front-row seats."

"Wow! How did you manage that?" I asked with admiration. "The tickets aren't even available yet."

"Oh, we have ways," Julia responded casually. "You know, now that Amanda's gone, we actually have an extra ticket. You could have it. If you want."

My heart gave a leap. *Front-row seats!* And I could have one?

But the Unicorns would have a total fit. "I don't know." I hesitated.

Julia sighed. "Come on, Kimberly. I saw you this afternoon with the Unicorns. You looked like you wanted to be just about anywhere instead of with them."

Was it that obvious?

"I know they're popular and everything, but face it. They're seventh-graders. They just haven't matured yet."

Julia was right. It wasn't just the singing in the mall or the stupid teenybopper T-shirts or the prank phone calls. It was the way Jessica and Lila always had to one-up the other, the way Ellen just sort of went along with the crowd, the way Mandy was always chomping on her gum. That kind of stuff never used to bother me. But well, I guess I've really grown up in the last year.

Julia sighed again. "I don't want to pressure you, Kimberly. But why don't you just accept the ticket and hang out with us at the concert. See what we're like. If you like what you see, we'll throw a big party sometime after the concert and we'll make it official. You'll be an Eight. If you don't like what you see, well, then I guess you go back to the Unicorns. No hard feelings."

"OK," I heard myself say. *OK? Did I really say OK?*

"OK!" Julia responded with a laugh. "Well, I guess we'll see you tomorrow, Kimberly."

"OK," I said again. Then we hung up.

I took a deep breath. It wasn't like I was *joining* the Eights. I was just going to hang out with them at one concert. What was so terrible about that?

I'd have to be a total idiot to turn down front-row seats to the Johnny Buck concert. The Unicorns would understand that, wouldn't they?

"Hey, Kimberly. What's up?" I ran into Ellen in the school parking lot. Her mom had dropped her off at the same time my dad had dropped me off.

"Hi, Ellen. Not much," I replied, trying to sound nonchalant.

This was a good opportunity to bring up the subject of the Eights and their front-row tickets to the Johnny Buck concert. I mean, wouldn't it be better to tell just one of the Unicorns rather than the whole group? That way they couldn't all gang up on me.

The only problem was I wasn't really sure how I should word it. I also wasn't sure Ellen was the one I wanted to tell.

Sure, she's the president of the Unicorn Club. But she's also the one who'd be most likely to take it personally. She's been especially sensitive since her parents split up, and she'd see this as some huge betrayal. Which it wasn't. It was just one concert with the Eights. That was all.

"You're really quiet," Ellen commented as we walked into the school.

"I'm just thinking about stuff," I said, shrugging.

"What stuff?" Ellen peered at me curiously.

"Just eighth-grade stuff," I said casually. "You wouldn't understand."

Ellen's blue eyes grew large. "Oh," she said knowingly. "*Eighth*-grade stuff. Well, excu-u-use me! I'll just slink away to the seventh-grade lockers here and leave you alone."

I rolled my eyes. This was exactly why I didn't tell her what was really on my mind. She just took things so personally sometimes.

Come to think of it, Lila and Jessica might not be good choices either. They were both easily offended too.

That left Mandy.

Mandy wasn't a bad choice. She always tried to see the best in people. She'd see that I just wanted a good seat at the concert, that I wasn't out to make anyone mad.

I usually saw Mandy alone when we passed between our second- and third-period classes. I'd catch her then.

I waited by the stairs next to Mr. Bowman's room. Mandy always came up those stairs after second period. I checked my watch. She should be coming any minute now.

Yes, Mandy was definitely the one I wanted to

talk to about the concert. She was the one least likely to get all emotional on me, that was for sure.

Besides, I had a feeling that deep down she'd understand where I was coming from. She actually dropped out of the Unicorns for a while because she didn't like the way we were acting. It was right after I came back from Atlanta. I don't quite remember the details, but basically she thought everyone was acting really immature. Which is kind of funny because when you get right down to it, Mandy's just as immature as everyone else.

I checked my watch again. The bell was going to ring in just a couple of minutes. Where was Mandy?

The halls were thinning out as kids went into their classrooms. I could only wait a couple more minutes.

Just then I heard pounding. Someone was running up the stairs. I looked down at Mandy's reddish brown head. "There you are!" I said with relief. I wanted to get this over with.

But I was also nervous. My stomach felt like it did right before I had to give a speech in front of the whole class.

Mandy glanced up at me and grinned. "Oh. Were you waiting for me?" she asked breathlessly.

Now's your chance, I told myself. "Well, not exactly *waiting*," I said nonchalantly as we walked toward our classrooms. "It's just I always see you between classes. So when I didn't see you today, I was a little worried."

Mandy stopped outside her math class. "Oh, that's so sweet of you to worry," she said, cracking her gum.

"Yeah, well," I said, shrugging. *Come on, Kimberly. What are you waiting for? Tell her!* I ordered myself. But I just couldn't put the words together.

Mandy blew a huge bubble and sucked it back into her mouth. "I guess I'll see you later." She waved as she went to take her seat.

I was left standing in the hallway alone.

"We better leave at five A.M.," Jessica said as she took a bite of hamburger pizza.

It was lunchtime and we were gathered around the Unicorner, making plans for Saturday morning. Or I should say *they* were making plans. I was just sitting there, poking at my pizza, trying to get up the nerve to tell them I wouldn't be going with them.

"I don't know," Mandy objected. "I think we better make it earlier. Like four A.M."

"Four A.M.!" Lila gasped.

"You want to get good seats, don't you?" Ellen raised a questioning eyebrow.

"Yeah." Lila groaned. "I guess. What time does the store open anyway?"

"I don't know." Jessica shrugged. "Nine or ten."

"Well, why don't we just pitch a tent and camp out there the whole night?" Lila suggested.

Mandy, Jessica, and Ellen all squealed with delight. "Oh, yes!" Ellen cried. "Let's!"

"We can put the tent right in front of the door so no one can sneak in ahead of us," Jessica said with excitement.

"Yeah, everyone bring a sleeping bag and munchies," Mandy ordered.

"I can bring my portable stereo," Lila offered.

"Great!" Jessica responded. "Now, who's got Johnny's latest CD? Kimberly, you do, don't you? Can you bring it?"

Four expectant faces turned to me.

"Uh, well," I said nervously as I pulled the bits of hamburger off my pizza. "I don't think I'll be able to make it. But you guys can borrow my CD if you want," I offered.

Jessica frowned. "What do you mean you don't think you can make it?"

"Yeah. Weren't you the one who said if one of us had to get up at five o'clock in the morning, we *all* had to?" Lila demanded.

I couldn't look at them. Any of them. This wasn't the way I wanted to tell them. But I didn't have much choice.

I took a deep breath. *This is not a big deal*, I tried to tell myself. *Don't* make *it a big deal.*

"You see, the Eights have front-row seats to the concert," I explained. "And, well, they sort of invited me to go with them."

At first no one said anything. They just stared at me in disbelief.

Then Lila broke the silence. "Very funny, Kimberly." She laughed.

Mandy punched me on the arm. "Boy, you really had me going there, Kimberly," she said, grinning.

I cleared my throat. "Um, you guys?" I said softly. "I'm not kidding."

Lila's fork froze halfway to her mouth.

Jessica and Mandy glanced at each other, then frowned at me.

"Come on, it's *front-row seats!*" I defended myself. "Don't tell me if any of you were offered front-row seats, you wouldn't take them."

"Not if it was the Eights who was offering them," Jessica said coldly.

"Yeah, right," I said, rolling my eyes.

"What, are you like the new Eight now that Amanda's gone?" Mandy asked.

"No!" I said as though I'd never heard such an idea before.

"They wouldn't give you a ticket just like that," Lila said doubtfully. "There has to be more to it."

"Well," I admitted, glancing down at my plate. "Maybe they *did* ask if I wanted to join them—"

"I knew it!" Jessica shrieked.

"That's what Julia meant that day at the mall when she said, 'the offer still stands,'" Lila mimicked Julia's voice.

"Why are you guys making such a big deal out of this?" I asked, glancing around the table at each of them. "Yes, they invited me to join them, but that doesn't mean I'm going to. I'm just going to go to the concert with them. End of story." I picked up my pizza and took a bite.

But the Unicorns kept looking at me as if I were a criminal.

"Are you sure you wouldn't rather eat lunch with your new best friends, the Eight Times Eight Club?" Jessica asked in a mocking voice.

I threw my pizza down on my tray. "You know what? Maybe I *would* rather eat lunch with them. Especially if you guys are going to keep acting so immature!"

"Immature?" Lila widened her eyes.

"You think we're being immature?" Ellen sounded shocked.

"Yes," I responded. I had to be honest, didn't I? I mean, maybe if they knew how other people saw them, they'd act a little more sophisticated. "And not just now. All the time. It's like you guys don't *think* sometimes. You just *do* things."

"What things?" Ellen asked in a hurt voice.

"Well, like singing in the mall, for example," I said.

"What's wrong with singing?" Jessica wanted to know.

"Yeah, it just shows we're in a good mood," Mandy said, cracking her gum.

"It's embarrassing!" I cried. "A *lot* of the stuff you guys do is embarrassing. Like the way you constantly crack your gum, Mandy. Or the way you chased after Jimmy Lancer, Lila, even though everyone knew he'd never go out with a seventh-grader."

A few weeks ago Lila had pursued a ninth-grader like crazy, taking him out to dinner and buying him presents and everything.

"Oh, like you've never done anything stupid," Lila shot back. "Like you never chased after Herbert, who's only like in *college*. . . ."

"Never mind that," I said, my face heating up. I'd forgotten about that little incident during a Unicorn trip to a dude ranch. "I mean, I realize I'm a year older than the rest of you—"

"Oh, yes," Jessica said, shifting in her chair. "And that one year makes you *so* much more mature than the rest of us."

"It does!" I insisted.

Mandy rolled her eyes. "I can't wait until my birthday so I can be mature like Kimberly."

"Oh, me too," Jessica said sarcastically. "I've always wanted to be *mature*."

I slid back my chair. "There's obviously no

point in reasoning with you guys, so I guess I'll just see you later," I said, standing up.

"Fine," Jessica snapped.

"Sure," Lila added.

"Whatever," Ellen piped up.

"Kimberly! Over here!" Julia Abbott waved as I walked across the cafeteria.

I wasn't really planning to sit down with the Eights. I was just going to dump my tray and go hang out in the library or something until the Unicorns grew up. But hey, that could be a very long time. And since Julia had called me over, well, I decided to go.

As I set down my tray I glanced over at the Unicorner. I could almost see smoke coming out of my friends' ears.

"Hi, Kimberly!" seven voices chirped in unison.

I smiled in spite of myself. One thing about the Eights. They at least knew how to make a girl feel welcome.

Today the Eights were all wearing blue. Blue sweaters. Blue jeans. And blue ribbons in their hair.

"I hear you're coming to the concert with us," Kristin said, spearing a lettuce leaf with her fork.

Not one of the Eights was eating pizza today. They all had salads. I felt like a pig sitting there with my half-eaten slice. "Um, yeah," I said, covering my food with my napkin. "It was nice of you guys to invite me."

"Oh, we're just glad you could come!" Erica gushed.

"We are going to have, like, so much fun!" Susan said, shivering with excitement.

"Yeah, you know Jimmy Lancer, don't you, Kimberly?" Julia asked.

"Um, yeah," I said, hiding a smile. Funny how Jimmy Lancer's name could come up twice in one hour. I cleared my throat. "He goes to Sweet Valley High, doesn't he?"

"That's right." Marcy nodded, picking the tomatoes out of her salad. "He and his friends all have the row behind us at the concert."

"The whole row?" I asked incredulously. So much for the Unicorns getting first-row or even *second*-row seats at the concert. I couldn't help but feel a little smug about that.

"How did you guys get tickets already?" I asked. "I didn't think they went on sale until Saturday."

"They don't," Gretchen confirmed. "But Jimmy's brother is the manager at Great State Music." She grinned and glanced knowingly around the group. "So a bunch of tickets sort of got sold ahead of time."

I was about to say something about how cool that was when I noticed the Unicorns trooping past our table. They all shot dagger looks at me.

Once they were past, Julia snorted. "I'm sorry," she said, tossing her long blond hair. "I know they're your friends, Kimberly, so I shouldn't laugh. But the Unicorns are looking awfully pathetic these days."

"Yeah," Marcy agreed as she watched them dump their trays. "I think the Unicorns' reign at this school is just about over."

I practically choked. The Unicorns' reign was over? She had to be kidding!

"Yeah, remember last year?" Julia asked, looking at me. "Weren't there like ten of you then?"

"And now there are only four," Kristin said quietly.

Five, I thought. Including me. But I didn't have the courage to say it out loud.

I never really thought about it before. But the Eights were right. There *were* only half as many Unicorns this year as there had been other years. Were the Unicorns just about washed up at this school? Had they been replaced by the Eights?

Four

I actually felt sorry for the Unicorns. It was Saturday morning and it was *pouring* outside. My friends must have gotten drenched during their campout.

I was wandering around the mall by myself. I needed new tennis shoes and I knew better than to ask Jessica or Lila to come with me. Especially on a day they were camping out in the rain to get Johnny Buck tickets.

I sighed. I *hated* shopping by myself.

"Kimberly?" I heard a voice behind me. "Kimberly, is that you?"

I turned. "Tamara?" I asked with surprise.

She nodded.

"Wow," I said. Tamara Chase was a Unicorn last year. She used to have short brown hair, but it had grown way past her shoulders. She looked so different. Older. More sophisticated.

"I heard you were back. How are you?" Tamara asked, tucking a few strands of hair behind her ear.

"Good," I said, grinning. "Real good. How are you? How are Grace and Janet?"

Tamara shrugged. "I haven't seen either of them in a while, but I'm sure they're fine."

"You haven't seen them in a while?" I asked, surprised. That would be like me not seeing Jessica or Lila in a while.

Tamara shrugged. "We're all busy. You know how it is."

"You mean, you guys don't hang out together?" I asked incredulously.

"Well, we keep talking about getting together," Tamara explained. "We just never do it. We don't have any classes together and we all have different clubs and activities."

"Different activities?" I asked uncomfortably.

"Well, yeah," Tamara said, like I was a total idiot for asking. "I've got basketball, Grace has cheerleading; I don't even know what Janet's in."

I swallowed hard. It never occurred to me that Janet, Tamara, and Grace wouldn't stay close. I figured they'd form Unicorn Club Senior or something and when I graduated from middle school, I'd go right into it.

Tamara burst out laughing. "Don't look so

depressed, Kimberly. High school's great! Much better than middle school."

I tried to smile. "Yeah, well, I guess I'll find out for myself next year, right?"

"Right!" Tamara said, squeezing my arm.

"Listen, I'm trying to find a decent pair of tennis shoes. Do you want to come with me?" I asked hopefully.

Tamara looked apologetic. "I'm really sorry, Kimberly," she said. "But I'm meeting someone." She checked her watch. "In fact, I'm late. I've really got to run. But call me sometime. We'll do lunch or something."

We'll do lunch? That sounded like the ultimate brush-off.

"Look, you guys! It's Kimberly!" Julia Abbott said with a smile. She and the other Eights were just coming into the mall as I was leaving.

"Hi, Kimberly!" seven voices chirped like I was a long-lost cousin or something. I noticed they weren't all dressed identically today. Most of them were wearing black pants, but Julia was wearing a red sweater, Marcy was wearing a white blouse with a blue sweater, Carmen and Gretchen were wearing Sweet Valley Middle School sweatshirts, and I couldn't really see what Susan, Kristin, and Erica were wearing under their red eight-ball jackets.

I switched my shoe box to my other arm. "Hi, you guys," I said as they surrounded me.

"What are you doing here?" Gretchen asked in a friendly voice.

"I, um, needed new tennis shoes," I responded.

"Really?" Susan said, like it was the most interesting thing in the world. "Can we see what you bought?"

"Um, yeah. OK," I agreed. We moved away from the doors so we weren't blocking people and I took the lid off my box.

At first no one said anything. They all just looked at each other.

Great! I had obviously picked the most dorky pair of shoes in the whole store. I *hated* shopping by myself!

I was about ready to take my shoes back to the store when I noticed every single one of the Eights was smiling. "What?" I asked nervously. I hated being on the outside of a joke even more than I hated shopping by myself.

"You bought the exact same pair of tennis shoes that we wear," Erica informed me.

I looked down at their feet. Erica was right. It wasn't just that I chose the same *brand* of shoe they wore—I chose the same style *and* the same color.

The Eights all giggled. "What did I tell you, Kimberly?" Julia said knowingly. "You're *destined* to be one of us."

I shivered. *Was* I destined to be an Eight? I had to admit, it was pretty weird that I picked out the same exact shoes that they wear.

"Hey, why don't you come hang out with us," Marcy offered, running a hand through her long red hair.

Hang out with them? Well, it wasn't like I had anything better to do. "OK," I said with a smile.

"No, Kimberly. Slide the cue stick along your finger," Julia instructed. "If you just shoot, you could tear a hole in the fabric."

The Eights and I were hanging out at Fun City, this place at the mall that has billiard tables, Ping-Pong tables, and pinball machines. I hadn't hung out here before. I always thought this place was more of a high-school hangout. But apparently the Eights came here all the time.

"Come on, Kimberly," Carmen urged. "Try it again."

I set my hand down on the soft green fabric of the billiard table. I curled my index finger around the cue stick. Then I pulled back, slid the stick along my third finger, and hit the white ball. It went a whole three inches.

"Not bad." Julia nodded, folding her arms across her chest.

"You'll get it, Kimberly," Marcy said with encouragement. "Just keep practicing."

The Eights were really into Eight Ball, so they were trying to teach me. But first I had to learn how to hold a cue stick and how to hit the ball. I had no idea it was all so complicated.

"Hey, guys!" A really cute guy strolled over to their table. A really cute *older* guy. "Is this the new Eight?" he asked, leaning on his cue stick and smiling at me.

My face flushed. The guy had wavy blond hair, nice green eyes, and a friendly smile that seemed to be just for me.

"It's not official yet," Erica told him. "For now Kimberly's just hanging out with us."

I had to give them credit. They weren't pressuring me to join them or anything. It was just like Erica said: I was only hanging out with them.

"Kimberly, this is Greg Dahl," Susan informed me. "He's a sophomore at Sweet Valley High."

A *sophomore?* My eyes nearly popped out of my head. The Eights hung with sophomores? But I played it really cool. "Hi, Greg," I said, as though I hung with sophomores all the time.

"I'm just about to start a game with Matsen over there. Why don't you come on over and bring me some luck," Greg said, smiling at me. He could've been in a toothpaste commercial.

"Troy's here?" Erica blushed.

"Erica and Troy Matsen are kind of an item," Susan whispered in my ear.

"Really?" I said, glancing at Troy.

He was wearing black jeans and a black T-shirt. He shook his curly dark hair out of his face. "Come over here, Wench!" he said coolly.

"I love it when he calls me wench!" Erica whispered to the rest of us. Then she hurried over to him.

Greg held out his hand to me. "Are you coming, Kimberly?" he asked.

"I don't know." I hesitated. "I'm not very good at pool." But I *wanted* to go. I wanted to go very much.

"You don't have to play," Greg said with a shrug. "Just come and watch."

"Well, OK," I agreed.

Erica scooted over to make room for me on the bench beside her. "Are you having fun?" she asked.

"Yeah," I said, smiling. I really *was* having fun.

"Well, we hang out here almost every day after school," Erica told me. "You can join us anytime."

I had to admit, the Eights were a lot cooler than I ever imagined.

"I just thought you should know, we managed to get fifth-row seats at the Johnny Buck concert," Jessica said, flipping her hair over her shoulder.

It was Monday morning and she was waiting for me by my locker.

"*Fifth* row, huh?" I said, spinning the dial on my lock. Poor Unicorns.

"Well, fifth row is much better than first row," Jessica rationalized as she leaned against the locker next to mine. "You get a better view."

I grabbed the books I'd need for my morning classes. I decided not to reply. Jessica could think whatever she wanted.

"I just can't believe you're doing this," Jessica said, shaking her head. "I can't believe you're choosing the Eights over us."

"What's so hard to believe?" someone behind me asked suddenly.

I jumped. I didn't realize Julia and Carmen were standing there.

"Yeah, Kimberly has a good time when she's with us," Carmen piped in. She turned to me and smiled. "Hi, Kimberly," she said sweetly.

"Hi," I responded. Carmen was right. I *did* have a good time with the Eights. But I felt uncomfortable saying so in front of Jessica.

"Well, she has a good time when she's with us too!" Jessica said, holding her ground.

Julia snorted. "I'm sure she does," she said with a sidelong glance at Carmen.

"We'll see you later, Kimberly," Carmen told

me. The two of them burst out laughing as they walked away.

Jessica's face was crimson. "How can you stand those two?" she shrieked.

"They're not so bad," I said calmly. "Once you get to know them."

"I know all I need to know about the Eights," Jessica spat out. "And I would've thought you did too, Kimberly."

Five

You shouldn't judge people by what other people say about them. That was what I was thinking during history class on Tuesday. We were supposed to be working on our work sheets, but at the moment the causes of the Revolutionary War just couldn't compare to my own problems.

When I first moved back to Sweet Valley and found out about the Eight Times Eight Club, I didn't really have an opinion about them. I just went along with what the Unicorns thought.

But I didn't really know any of the Eights. I sort of knew Julia from when we were little. We used to play together, go to each other's birthday parties, that kind of thing. But as we got older we sort of drifted apart. She and Amanda Harmon became best friends. And I met Janet Howell and the others and we formed the Unicorn Club.

The Unicorn Club was a lot different then. It was made up of sixth-, seventh- and eighth-graders, not mostly seventh-graders and one eighth-grader. Everybody in all three grades looked up to us, wanted to be us. In all honesty, though, I thought people admired the Eights more than they admired the Unicorns now.

In fact, I wondered whether people saw the Unicorn Club as a *seventh*-grade club. A seventh-grade club with one poor pathetic eighth-grader.

The bell rang, interrupting my thoughts. "Remember, people!" Mr. Nydick said, raising his hands to get everyone's attention. "There will be an exam on this material on Friday."

Bruce Patman groaned.

"But Mr. Nydick," Carmen argued. "The Johnny Buck concert is Saturday night."

Mr. Nydick blinked. "So?"

"So don't you think it's like sacrilegious or something to have a test so close to the day he's performing?" Carmen asked in a serious voice.

Nice try, I thought, grinning at Julia. But there was no way Mr. Nydick was going to change his test.

"If you all spend time between now and Friday studying, you'll do fine. Then you can enjoy your concert without worrying about your grade on the test. Which, by the way, will count for about twenty percent of your grade this quarter," Mr. Nydick told everyone.

"So Bruce Patman is having a preconcert party on Saturday night," Julia announced.

It was after school on Tuesday and we were hanging out at Fun City. Marcy and Erica were in the middle of a game of Eight Ball. The rest of us were clustered around Julia, reading the computer-generated party invitation in her hand. We had all gotten one.

"What do you say, guys?" she asked, glancing over her shoulder at us. "Do we want to do this thing or not?"

"I heard Bruce and Jake Hamilton talking after history," Gretchen offered. "Bruce said he's planning to play every song Johnny ever recorded. He's going to start with his first one and work through his latest CD."

"That sounds cool," I said. Bruce's parents are loaded. His family lives in a huge mansion, and his parties are always really fun.

"Yeah," Carmen agreed. "But remember, Bruce is still just an eighth-grader."

"True." Julia nodded. "Do we really want to go to an *eighth*-grade party?" She made it sound like we were more than eighth-graders ourselves.

"Have you talked to Troy?" Carmen asked

Susan. "Is anybody from Sweet Valley High having a party before the concert?"

A high-school party? "Do you guys get invited to high-school parties?" I asked incredulously. The Unicorns always got invited to the coolest parties, but we'd *never* been invited to a high-school party.

"Sure." Julia shrugged like it was no big deal. "We go to high-school parties all the time."

Wow, I thought. I was really impressed.

"Some kids are having parties *after* the concert," Susan said. "But I don't know of any *before* the concert."

"Well, maybe we could go to Bruce's party before the concert and one of the high-school parties after the concert," Gretchen said diplomatically.

Marcy wrinkled her nose. "I don't know if my mom will let me go out after the concert," she admitted.

I was really glad she said that. I wasn't sure my mom would let me go out after the concert either.

Just then Greg and Troy and some other high-school guys came in. All heads immediately swiveled in their direction.

"Hi, Troy!" Erica giggled.

"Hey, Wench!" Troy responded. He snapped his fingers. "Come on over here."

Erica dropped her cue stick and ran right over,

even though she and Marcy were in the middle of a game.

"Why don't you *all* come over here," another dark-haired boy said. It sounded like an order. "Improve the scenery a little."

I blushed. But none of the Eights needed a second invitation. They all jumped up and ran over to the boys as though they'd been waiting for them all along.

Maybe the Eights were used to hanging out with high-school guys, but I wasn't. I was excited to be included in a group of high-school guys, but nervous too.

Greg racked up the balls and Troy broke them with a loud bang. The fifteen ball rolled into one corner pocket and the eleven ball was close to the other corner. "I get stripes," Troy announced. He walked around to the corner where the fifteen ball had gone in and shot the eleven ball into the opposite corner pocket.

Greg frowned. He turned to me. "I'm not worried. Not with Kimberly, my good luck charm, cheering me on."

Julia nudged me and giggled. I felt my face turn about seven shades of red. Greg called *me* his good luck charm?

On the next ball Troy accidentally shot the eight ball in, which meant Greg won the game.

Greg shook the hair out of his face and grinned.

"What'd I tell you? My good luck charm."

"Ooo, Kimberly!" Carmen squealed.

My face felt even hotter. I had to bite my lip to keep from beaming like a total fool.

I figured he'd ask me to play next. Or maybe Troy would ask Erica if she wanted to play. But they didn't. They just started another game.

In fact, they played four more games while the eight of us just sat there and watched them. It got a little boring after a while. At least for me. But the Eights watched every play as though it was a matter of life and death. Maybe I just needed to learn more about the game?

"I think Greg likes you, Kimberly," Julia said.

It was almost dinnertime and the Eights were walking me home from the mall.

"I don't know," I said modestly. I could feel my face heating up again.

"He does!" Gretchen insisted.

I *hoped* he liked me. It was kind of hard to tell since he paid more attention to his game than to me.

"Maybe you and Greg can double with me and Troy sometime," Erica offered.

"Sure." I tried to sound nonchalant, but my heart started beating hard. I pictured all four of us on a date, at a restaurant with candles and table-cloths. (These were high-school guys, after all.)

Greg would turn to me, look into my eyes . . .

I shivered. I still couldn't believe I was actually considering going out with a *high-school* guy. But I was in eighth grade. Greg was in ninth. That's only one year difference. It was just the difference between high school and middle school seemed so big. It would be *too* big a difference for someone like Jessica or Mandy. But not for me.

"There's my house," I said, feeling disappointed that it was almost time to say good-bye to the Eights. I really had fun when I was with them.

"It's big," Gretchen said, wide-eyed.

"Big enough to host a really cool party," Susan put in.

"Shhh!" Julia nudged her. "There's her dad."

I looked. Julia was right. My dad was sitting on the porch steps. He was pouring milk into a rolled-up newspaper. Uh-oh. Magic again.

"Hi, Kimberly!" He waved.

Carmen and Erica giggled.

"Hi, Dad," I mumbled, feeling embarrassed.

Dad got up and came toward us with the milk and the newspaper. *No, Dad,* I thought, cringing. *Please don't!* It was one thing for him to try his stupid magic tricks in front of the Unicorns, but in front of the Eights?

"Well, who are all these pretty young ladies?" Dad asked, smiling at them.

I saw Kristin and Erica exchange a look.

"They're my new friends," I muttered. I stared wide-eyed at my dad, sending him an ESP message. *Please don't embarrass me.*

But I don't think he got it. "New friends?" Dad's whole face lit up. I knew exactly what he was thinking. New victims for him to practice his magic on.

"Hey, Mr. Haver," Susan said with a smirk. "Wouldn't you rather drink that out of a cup?"

Dad glanced down at the newspaper in his hand, then grinned at Susan. "I'm glad you asked that," he said with a gleam in his eye.

I groaned. There was no stopping him now.

"Kimberly may have mentioned I'm an amateur magician." Dad shrugged modestly.

"No," Julia responded with skepticism.

"No?" Dad looked surprised. He had to be kidding! He didn't really expect me to be telling people about his magic, did he?

"Well, let me show you this trick I've been working on."

"Dad!" I said in a warning voice.

"Relax, Kimberly. It's not going to take very long." He turned to Julia and the other Eights. "I'm going to make this pitcher of milk *disappear*," he said with enthusiasm.

As he slowly rolled the newspaper into a cone I glanced nervously at the Eights. Julia was tapping her foot. Carmen was yawning. The others all had bored expressions on their faces. "Come on, Dad," I said, feeling uncomfortable. "Hurry up."

"You can't rush these things, Kimberly," Dad said as he began pouring the milk into his newspaper cone. I could see little drops of milk dripping from the point at the bottom.

"OK!" Dad said cheerfully as he handed the empty pitcher to Marcy. "Would you hold that for me, please?"

Marcy raised an eyebrow, but she took it.

"Now, with a wave of my hand and a few magic words . . ." Dad paused dramatically. "Alacazooie!"

"Alacazooie?" Susan mouthed. She looked confused.

"You will see that the milk has disappeared!" Dad cried as he whipped open the newspaper cone. Milk spewed everywhere! On shirts, pants, and shoes.

"Ew!" Julia wrinkled her nose as she stepped back.

"My hair!" Marcy gasped. Beads of milk dotted her red hair.

I was never so embarrassed in my entire life. "Thanks a lot, Dad!" I said angrily. Tears sprang to my eyes. The Eights would never want me in their club after this.

I didn't know what to do. So I ran up to the house and slammed the door. I didn't even say good-bye. How could I ever show my face at school again?

*   *   *

Apologize. That's what I had to do.

First thing Wednesday morning I headed for the downstairs bathroom. The Eights "office" here at school. But along the way I ran into the Unicorns. I suddenly realized I hadn't really seen them all week. We all came to an abrupt stop.

Mandy was the first to break the silence. "Kimberly! Hi," she said brightly.

"How are you?" Ellen asked, hugging her notebook to her chest.

Jessica and Lila just stared at me.

"Listen," I said, running a hand through my hair. "I really don't have time to stay and chat right now."

"Oh, are you running off to a meeting with your *mature* friends?" Jessica asked sarcastically.

I sighed. "If you're wondering whether I'm meeting the Eights, yes, I am. But I don't see why you guys always have to make such a big deal about it. If you gave Julia and them half a chance, you'd see they're not so bad."

"Yeah, right," Mandy said, rolling her eyes.

"I'll see you guys later," I said, ignoring Mandy. *I*, at least, was going to be *mature* about this.

"Wait!" Lila grabbed my arm. "Today's our day at the day care center."

I blinked. "So?"

"So are you coming with us or not?" Mandy wanted to know.

"I don't think so," I said as I started walking toward the Eights' bathroom.

"But you said you would," Ellen said in a whiny voice. She and the other Unicorns trailed along behind me. "Mrs. Willard is expecting *all* of us."

"Well, I changed my mind," I said impatiently. If things went well with the Eights this morning, I hoped I'd be invited back to Fun City with them this afternoon. That sounded like a lot more fun than hanging around a stupid day care center. Volunteering there had never been my idea of a great time in the first place.

"So are you quitting the Unicorns now or what?" Mandy asked bluntly.

I stopped. I felt my stomach tighten. "W-W-Why would you ask me that?" I stammered.

"Because you're not acting like you want to be a Unicorn anymore." Jessica stomped her foot.

"I don't know what you guys are talking about," I said, shifting nervously. "But I've really got to go. We'll talk about this later, OK?"

The last thing I needed right now was to get into a big confrontation with the Unicorns. First I had to find out whether Dad's stupid magic trick had cost me my friendship with the Eights.

"Hi, Kimberly!" seven voices chorused as I entered the bathroom. The Eights were lined up at the mirror, combing their hair and putting on makeup.

Julia giggled. "What's the matter, Kimberly? You look so nervous."

"Well," I said, wringing my hands. "I wasn't sure . . . I mean, I didn't know if . . ." I was blathering like a total idiot.

Julia and Carmen exchanged a look in the mirror. "You weren't sure whether we still wanted to hang out with you after your dad practically drowned us?" Carmen asked.

"Sort of," I admitted.

"Relax, Kimberly," Gretchen said sympathetically. "We *all* have parents."

"Yeah, my dad tells stupid jokes," Susan said, rolling her eyes. She handed her lipstick to Erica.

Erica spread pink lipstick across her lips. "Yeah, and my dad sings Broadway show tunes," she said, handing the lipstick to Carmen.

"He's totally off-key," Marcy informed me.

I laughed along with everyone else. What a relief! Frankly, I was pretty sure my dad was the most embarrassing father of all, but it was nice of the Eights to be so forgiving.

Carmen handed me Erica's lipstick. "You're one of us now, Kimberly," she said seriously. "We're not going to judge you by the bizarre things someone in your family does."

"Yeah, that would be totally shallow," Julia put in.

I uncapped the lipstick and stepped up to the mirror. *One of us*, Carmen had said. I squinted at my reflection in the mirror. Was I one of them?

I thought I was just hanging out with them. But maybe I *was* becoming one of them. If I was, where did that leave the Unicorns?

Six

"You look great!" Julia grinned as I turned around in front of the full-length mirror. "Just like a real Eight."

It was Thursday morning and we were hanging out in the Eights' office before school. I was trying on Julia's official club jacket.

Erica and Susan walked around behind me. Erica tugged the jacket down in back. Susan puffed up the shoulders.

"It looks like you and Julia wear the same size," Kristin commented.

I looked at Julia and she smiled at me. "Just say the word, Kimberly, and we'll order a jacket just like it for you," she said cheerfully.

"Well, I'll have to save a little money first," I replied, slipping off the jacket and handing it to Julia.

"We could still order you a jacket now," Julia said, putting on her jacket. "It won't come in for several weeks and you won't have to pay until it comes in."

"I'll think about it," I said, stalling for time. I was having a good time with the Eights, but ordering one of their jackets seemed so, I don't know . . . *final*. Like I'd definitely decided I was joining the Eights and quitting the Unicorns.

I have to admit, I did kind of like that idea. I mean, the Eights were so cool. So sophisticated. So much *fun*. But I'd been a Unicorn since the very beginning. Could I really walk away just like that?

The bell rang and we gathered up our books. As we left the bathroom we nearly collided with Mandy. She did a double take when she saw me.

"You look just like them!" Mandy accused me.

I touched my gold hoop earrings self-consciously. Today was black pants and hoop earrings day. When Julia told me that yesterday, I was thrilled to be included in their dressing plans. But seeing Mandy today made me feel a little funny about it.

"She *is* like us," Julia told Mandy, draping an arm over my shoulders.

"Yeah, so why shouldn't she look like us?" Erica added, her hands on her hips.

Mandy was wearing a green army jacket with tons of pins all over it. It was *kind of* cool, but it was also an army jacket. The Eights didn't wear army jackets.

Mandy shrugged. "It's your life." She stared hard at me. "But tell me something. Do they make you leave your brain at the door when you hang out with them?"

I frowned. Mandy did her own thing regardless of what people thought. It was a quality I'd always admired in her before. But today it ticked me off. What was wrong with a group of friends dressing alike?

"Grow up, Mandy!" I muttered as I headed off to first period with the Eights.

"So we've decided?" Julia asked the Eights at lunch on Thursday. "We're going to go to Bruce's party before the concert on Saturday?"

I glanced around at the others. Kristin and Erica nodded.

"Sure. Why not?" Carmen said, shoving a forkful of lettuce into her mouth.

"It's not like any of us can go to one of the high-school parties after the concert," Susan said glumly.

"Should we introduce Kimberly as the new Eight at Bruce's party?" Julia asked everyone.

My heart stopped. *Introduce me as the new Eight?* I hadn't realized I'd officially decided to join them yet.

"Yeah, let's!" Erica nodded enthusiastically.

"We definitely should make a public announcement," Carmen said, smiling at me.

But I wasn't sure I was *ready* to make a public announcement yet! Especially not at Bruce's party. The Unicorns would probably be there. And, well, don't you have to quit one club before you can join another?

"I don't know, you guys," Marcy said as she bit into an apple. "Getting a new member is kind of a big deal. Don't you think we should have a party of our own to make the announcement?"

"Yes!" I spoke up quickly. But then I felt a little embarrassed. "I mean, I don't want to tell you guys you *have* to have a party for me or anything," I assured them. "But joining you is kind of a big thing for me." A *really* big thing. "And, well, I don't know, it just seems like announcing it at someone else's party would be . . ." My voice trailed off. I didn't quite know how to finish that sentence without sounding tacky.

Julia slapped her palm against the table. "You're absolutely right, Kimberly."

"Absolutely," Carmen echoed, patting my arm. "That was really thoughtless of us."

"Of course we'll have a separate party just for you," Gretchen promised.

"Wow," I said. "Really?" Even though I basically said I wanted them to throw a party for me, I was totally overwhelmed by their willingness to do it.

"How about we do it next weekend?" Susan suggested.

Julia wrinkled her nose. "I don't know. Do you think we can really pull together a party in just a week?"

The Unicorns could, I thought. *The Unicorns could plan a party in less than a day.* But there was probably a lot more to an Eights party than there was to a Unicorn party.

I glanced over my shoulder at the Unicorner. I had to admit, the Unicorns were acting like civilized people today. No napkin throwing or obvious gum chomping. They were just sitting there talking.

I wondered what they were talking about. Could they be talking about me? Did they miss me?

I wouldn't say I was exactly missing them. But when you've been friends with people as long as I've been friends with the Unicorns, well, it's hard not to think about them at all. No matter how immature they are.

Lately I'd been remembering all kinds of weird things the Unicorns and I had done together. Like that stupid beauty pageant we had all entered a few weeks ago. Or rather, *they* all entered. I got cold feet at the last minute. And Mandy, who all along had said beauty pageants were sexist and degrading to women, went on in my place. She ended up winning first place!

"What are you smiling about, Kimberly?" Carmen asked.

"What?" I asked, shaking myself back to the present. "Oh, I'm thinking about this great party you guys are going to throw for me." Which reminded me of something else about the Unicorns. When I came back from Atlanta, *they* didn't throw a party for me. In fact, I don't think they've *ever* thrown a party just for me.

"We should also decide who's going to take Amanda's place as president of the Eights," Marcy reminded everyone.

"We agreed we're going to do speeches, right?" Gretchen asked, glancing around the table.

"That's right," Julia replied. She turned to me. "You could prepare a speech too, if you want to be president."

I had a shot at being president of the Eights? I had virtually no chance of ever being president of the Unicorns! Ellen would remain president all year and next year I'd be at Sweet Valley High.

"What kind of speech?" I asked, mulling over the possibility in my head.

"Just something about what the club means to you and what sorts of things you want us to do the rest of the year," Carmen responded.

"Yeah, then we'll vote by secret ballot to determine our new president," Susan put in.

I was amazed. It was just like a *real* presidential election. As opposed to the immature election the Unicorns held at the beginning of the year. I wasn't here then, but I'd heard about it.

It started out as a dare war between Jessica and Lila. One of them stole Mrs. Arnette's hairnet. Another of them stole Mr. Clark's hairpiece. It was like whoever did the stupidest thing got to be president.

Eventually they decided Mandy should be president because she was the only one who wasn't making a total fool out of herself. But then she quit the Unicorns and somehow *Ellen* ended up president. Ellen, who couldn't make a decision on her own to save her life! Like I said. I wasn't here then, so don't blame me.

One thing was certain. The Eights' way of doing things was so much more mature.

"All right, Kimberly!" Julia applauded from the bench where she was sitting. She had her history book open in her lap.

We were hanging out at Fun City after school. It was sort of a combination eight-ball game and study fest for our history test tomorrow. I was personally more interested in the game, especially since I had just sunk another ball.

"You're really getting the hang of this," Carmen observed. Carmen was my opponent.

"Yeah," I said, flipping my hair behind my shoulder. "Eight Ball is pretty fun."

"Well, what other game would the Eight Times Eight Club be into?" Carmen asked.

We all laughed.

"OK, Kimberly," Julia spoke up. "Since you sank another ball, you have to answer another question. Who was Dr. Benjamin Church?"

The Eights watched me to see if I knew. I thought back to the work sheet that listed all the important people from that time period. "Was he the guy who spied on us for the British?" I asked.

"Tell me more," Julia said, bringing her legs up under her.

I thought hard. "He was the *first* guy caught spying for the British," I said confidently.

"That's right." Julia grinned.

"Yeah, there was that other guy too," Carmen pointed out. "Benedict Arnold."

"Wasn't he a leader or something?" Marcy asked.

"I think so," Julia said, flipping through the pages. "He's more famous than this Church guy is."

I really liked how the Eights studied together. Either we'd all do really well or we'd all fail. The Unicorns hardly ever studied together.

"OK, Kimberly, you get another turn," Carmen reminded me.

"I know," I said, surveying the table. I still had five more balls to shoot. Carmen only had three.

The six ball was in line to the corner pocket. I picked up my cue stick, took aim, and totally missed the cue ball. I cringed.

"Scratch!" Carmen and Erica said in unison.

"Tough break," came a voice behind me.

I whirled around. Greg and Troy and several other cute high-school boys were standing there! I wanted to drop through the floor and die! "Hey, I did manage to get two in the pockets," I said, trying to make light of the situation.

Greg smiled. "Well, that's a start," he said encouragingly.

"Yeah, she also got two of mine in," Carmen teased.

"Tsk tsk." Greg shook his head, then draped an arm across my shoulders. "Maybe I'll have to give you some lessons," he said teasingly.

My face burned. I tried to give him my most flirtatious smile. "Maybe you will."

Carmen grinned at me. Julia gave me a thumb's-up sign. And all eight of us followed Greg over to where the guys were playing.

But I never did get any lessons. First Greg played a game with Troy. Then he played with Jimmy. Then he played with some other guy who had just walked in. None of the Eights knew him and nobody bothered to introduce him.

"You've hogged the table long enough, Dahl," Jimmy Lancer said finally.

I sat up a little straighter, sure that Jimmy was going to invite one of us to play. But he didn't. Instead he nodded to the guy none of us knew. "You want to break or should I?" he asked.

"Go ahead," the guy responded.

I leaned in toward the Eights. "Does it ever bother you guys that we never get to play?" I asked.

Seven faces stared at me blankly. "What do you mean?" Julia asked.

"Well, when the boys are around, they just sort of expect us to sit there and watch them play."

"So?" Susan shrugged.

I thought about Mandy, who sometimes wore a T-shirt that said, "Women Belong in the House . . . and the Senate." She would have a total fit about the way we were letting these guys walk all over us. Even if they *were* high-school guys.

"So don't you guys want to play?" I asked.

Erica shrugged. "It's more fun to watch *them* play," she said, grinning.

"Jimmy Lancer gets this look of deep concentration," Julia said.

"Yeah, I love the way he blows his hair out of his face right before he takes a shot," Marcy put in. She blew her bangs out of her face to demonstrate.

We all laughed. She looked just like Jimmy when she did that.

I had to admire the Eights for not getting all bent out of shape about being ignored. They even joked about it. Mandy never jokes about things like equality between the sexes.

"Well, it was nice to see you girls again." Jimmy nodded at all of us.

"Do we have a date tomorrow night, Wench?" Troy asked Erica.

Erica grinned. "We sure do."

I bit my lip, wondering whether Greg would ask *me* for a date. But he and Jimmy started chatting about some stupid boxing match they'd seen on TV as they made their way to the door. He didn't even say good-bye to me.

"I'll meet you here at six-thirty," Troy told Erica. "Don't be late."

"I won't be," Erica promised.

I was surprised Troy wasn't picking Erica up at her house. Isn't that the way real dates worked?

"Remember, if you're late, I'll start playing with the guys and I won't leave until the game is over."

"But then we might miss the movie," Erica protested.

Troy shrugged. "So don't be late," he repeated. He turned to the door. "Hey, Lancer! Dahl! Wait up!"

Poor Erica. Troy didn't even sound like he cared whether they had a date or not.

But if she was upset, she didn't show it. "Do you guys have to get home or do you want to grab something to eat?" she asked.

Gretchen checked her watch. "I could probably stay."

"Me too," Marcy chimed in.

Everyone looked at me.

It was almost time for dinner. "Well, if I call
home and tell my folks I'm going to be late, I
probably could stay."

"Great!" Julia grinned.

We all gathered up our things and headed out
into the mall. "Where are we going to eat?" I
asked. "Casey's?"

The Eights all looked at me like I'd suggested
jumping out of an airplane without a parachute.
"Casey's?" Carmen asked incredulously. "Are
you kidding?"

"What's wrong with Casey's?" I asked. Aside
from the fact the Unicorns went there all the time
and we might run into them.

"Nothing, if you don't mind getting fat,"
Marcy said, patting her stomach.

"Yeah, you can gain ten pounds just walking
past that place," Gretchen informed me.

"Aren't you on a diet, Kimberly?" Carmen
asked with surprise.

"Uh, no," I said, glancing self-consciously at
my middle. *Should I be on one?* I wondered.

"We've been dieting all year," Kristin informed me.

"You have?" I asked incredulously. "*All* of you

are dieting?" But none of them was at all heavy.

"Sure," Susan replied, patting her thighs. "I don't know about you, Kimberly, but I don't intend to start high school with thunder thighs like these."

I bit my lip. I had gym with Susan, so I knew for a fact my thighs were actually heavier than hers.

I sighed. Didn't the Eights *ever* eat things like ice cream or pizza?

"We usually eat at The Salad Bowl when we come to the mall," Marcy informed me.

"Oh," I said, trying to hide my disappointment. "Well, that sounds fine."

As we walked past Casey's, I caught a glimpse of the Unicorns clustered around a table inside. Lila's back was to me, so I couldn't see her. But Mandy was blowing another one of her stupid bubbles. Ellen was laughing into her hand. And Jessica was shoving a heaping spoonful of ice cream into her mouth.

I felt my stomach rumble. That ice cream sure looked good.

Oh, stop it! I told myself. It was only ice cream. *Kids* ate ice cream.

You're not a kid anymore, Kimberly Haver.

I had a hard time falling asleep that night. My body was tired, but my mind wouldn't turn off. I couldn't stop thinking about the Unicorns and the Eights.

I wanted to join the Eights. I mean, they're way more mature than the Unicorns are. They're concerned about things that I'm concerned about—like high school. And speaking of high school, joining the Eights now would mean I'd already have friends when I got there next year.

But part of me (a very *small* part) was actually going to *miss* the Unicorns. We'd had some really great times. Like the time we got stranded on an island. Or the time we tried to fill a dunk tank with Jell-O for the school carnival. Of course, those were things that happened *last* year, not this year.

The Unicorn Club has changed. Or maybe it's me who's changed. I've grown up and they haven't.

It's not their fault. I mean, they're seventh-graders. I'm an eighth-grader. You wouldn't think one year would make such a difference, but it does.

I sighed as I pulled my quilt up to my chin. I was going to have to tell the Unicorns I was moving on. I thought telling them I just wanted to go to the concert with the Eights was hard. Telling them I actually want to *join* the Eights was going to be ten times worse.

Seven

I heard voices. I opened my eyes. My bedroom was still dark, but there was a crack of light shining under my door. I checked my bedside clock. 2:32.

That's weird, I thought. *Who could be up at this time on a Friday morning?*

I kicked off my covers, swung my legs over the side of my bed, and padded over to the door. I opened it just a crack.

I heard my mother's frantic voice. "I'm calling nine-one-one!"

911? What was going on?

"Mom?" I called. "Dad?"

No answer.

I went out into the hall. The bright light blinded me for a minute, but my eyes soon adjusted. Where was everyone?

"We need an ambulance at Five-Forty-Five Sun Valley Road," my mom said briskly.

It sounded like she was on the phone. Downstairs.

I flew down the stairs two at a time. When I got to the bottom, I gasped. My dad was on the floor. He was lying on his side, panting. There was a wild animal look in his eyes.

"What's wrong?" I cried.

"Chest pain," Dad replied through gritted teeth.

"His name is Paul Haver," Mom told the person on the phone, but her eyes never left Dad. "He's fifty-three."

My heart was pounding. What was happening?

"Well, he said he wasn't feeling well," Mom explained. "He said he was going downstairs to get some 7UP. . . . What? Oh, not very long ago. Maybe ten minutes?"

Dad didn't look good at all. His lips were sort of bluish. His face was deathly pale. And rivers of sweat ran down his forehead, cheeks, and neck.

"This is . . . ridiculous, Barbara," Dad said, gasping for breath. "Just drive me . . . to the hospital. Don't bother . . . those people." He struggled to sit up, but the pain was too much.

"Just stay still!" Mom told Dad impatiently. "The ambulance is already on its way."

I swallowed hard. My hands felt as cold as ice. What was happening? Why did my dad look like that?

"Kimberly." Dad reached a sweaty hand out to me. "Go back . . . to bed, honey. . . . I'm fine . . . really," he panted.

I took a step back. "You don't look fine," I said in a small voice.

"No, he hasn't had any heart problems," Mom told the person on the phone. "He does have high cholesterol, though. And at his last physical his stress test wasn't completely normal. But the doctor said it wasn't completely abnormal either. So they didn't do anything about it."

Dad's face was getting bluer. He was struggling harder for breath. What if he passed out or something before the ambulance got here?

I wished Mom would get off the phone. I wanted her to do something. Make Dad better.

I went to the front window and moved the curtain so I could see outside. Where was that ambulance anyway? How long would it take an ambulance to get here?

I wrung my hands together. I didn't know what to do.

Dad was looking worse by the minute.
Come on, ambulance! Hurry up!

"Haver residence?" a police officer asked.

I nodded as I opened the door. Our house was already packed with people. There was one police officer, two paramedics, even two firefighters. All these people were clustered around my dad.

Somebody put an oxygen mask over his face.

Somebody else started an IV.

And a third person ripped open Dad's pajama top and put some white circles on his chest.

I just stood there, biting my lip and wishing this horrible nightmare was over.

"Pulse is about one hundred to one-twenty, Jim," one of the guys said. "And very irregular."

"How about a blood pressure reading?" someone else asked.

"Two hundred over one-twenty," a third voice chimed in.

Two hundred over one-twenty? Those sounded like pretty high numbers. What did they mean?

"Load and go," one of the paramedics announced.

My throat tightened as I watched the paramedics lift Dad to a stretcher and take him out of the house.

Mom grabbed her jacket from the brass rack in the corner and slipped it on over her nightgown. I grabbed my jacket and followed her outside. The cold night air made me shiver.

"You want to ride along with us?" one of the paramedics asked.

"Yes, please." Mom nodded. She didn't sound like herself.

After Dad was loaded into the back of the

ambulance, one of the paramedics helped Mom up into the back with him. I was going to climb in too, but the other paramedic stopped me. "Why don't you ride up in front with me?"

"OK," I said numbly. The guy hurried to the front of the ambulance and opened the door for me.

"My dad's going to be OK, isn't he?" I asked.

But the paramedic slammed my door shut without answering my question.

It felt weird being in an ambulance. There was a glass window behind me, so I could see what was going on with Dad, but I couldn't hear anything. The siren was blaring so loud, I probably wouldn't have been able to hear even if the window was open.

We were really cruising. Red lights swirled. Sirens screamed. Fortunately there wasn't much traffic at this hour. The one or two cars we *did* see pulled over to the right to let us pass.

I glanced over my shoulder again. I saw two guys leaning over Dad, but I couldn't tell what they were doing. A third guy was talking on a black telephone. My mom was sitting on the bench with her back to me.

I noticed a machine propped up on the bench across from my mom. It had a bunch of dials and a screen with a wavy green line running across it. I'd seen screens like that on TV shows about hospitals. Sometimes the wavy line suddenly turns into a straight line. The machine beeps. And everyone comes running.

If the wavy line became a straight line, these people would know what to do, wouldn't they?

I turned back around and watched the city pass in a blur. The ride was a little bumpy, but I didn't care. There was only one thing I *did* care about—that my dad would be OK.

"I'm feeling much better," Dad announced as he tried to sit up on the examining table. "Really, I am." We were in the emergency room. Dad had just had a bunch of tests and now we were waiting for the doctor to come back.

Mom gently pushed him back against the pillow. "That's good," she said. "But we're not leaving. Not until the doctor says we can."

My eyelids felt like there was sand in them. It was almost four o'clock in the morning. I don't think I'd even had two hours of sleep. But I wasn't about to conk out now.

I had to admit, Dad seemed a little better. Some of the color had returned to his cheeks and he didn't seem to be in so much pain anymore. But he still didn't look quite right. Maybe it was the ugly hospital light, I told myself, wanting to be optimistic.

"Well, at least take Kimberly home," Dad

insisted. "She doesn't need to be here. She's got school in the morning."

"I'm fine, Dad," I said, blinking the sleep out of my eyes. I wanted to be here. I felt like I *should* be here.

"Mr. and Mrs. Haver?" the doctor asked as he slid the curtain aside just far enough so he could walk through. He wore a white coat with a stethoscope hanging from his neck. He was about my dad's age. "I'm Dr. Alexander."

"Nice to meet you." Mom looked at him hopefully. "Was it a heart attack?"

The doctor closed the curtain again and came over to the examining table. "We don't know yet," he replied. "We'll have to repeat the enzyme test in about twelve hours. That's the only way we'll know for sure. But based on the symptoms you've been having, Mr. Haver, we're going to treat it like a heart attack and send you up to ICU."

"But he's doing well now, right?" I asked. I mean, you could look at Dad and *see* he was doing much better than he had been.

"He's stable," the doctor admitted. "We'll have to see how he does over the next twelve hours, though."

"You mean the pain could come back?" Mom asked, her face haggard with worry.

The doctor glanced down at my dad. "We'll

have to see what happens over the next twelve hours," he repeated gravely.

They moved Dad to the intensive care unit, or ICU, around four-thirty A.M. The rooms here were in a circle around the nurses' station. They all had glass fronts so you could see what was going on in each room. The whole area smelled like medicine and disinfectant and death. It wasn't a happy place at all. There was even a sign that said No Flowers.

What was my dad doing here with all these people who were dying?

Dad was hooked up to a machine that showed not only his heartbeat but his blood pressure too. There was a monitor in his room and out by the nurses so they could see right away if there was a problem.

There were tubes going into Dad's arm and his nose. And there were wires attached to the three circles that were still on his chest. But aside from all that, he was still my same old dad. He even smiled when Mom and I went in to see him. We were only allowed to see him for five minutes out of an hour, though.

"Well, this is pretty good," Mom said, trying to sound cheerful. "Look at all these people who are ready to wait on you."

Dad reached for Mom's hand. "I'd rather go home and let you wait on me," he said in a scratchy voice. His voice always sounds scratchy when he's tired.

Mom tried to smile, but I could see her lip quivering. She blinked several times, like she was trying not to cry.

"Why don't you two go home and get some rest," Dad suggested. "I'll be fine."

Mom shook her head. "I'm staying right here, Paul," she said, biting her lip.

She was going to burst into tears at any minute. I had to get her out of here before she totally lost it in front of Dad. "Come on, Mom," I said, grabbing her arm. "It's been five minutes. We should let Dad rest. We can come back in an hour."

She looked at me like she didn't even know me. Then she blinked a couple of times and glanced at the clock. "You're right, Kimberly," she said with a heavy sigh. She touched Dad's arm. "You should get some rest."

"You too," Dad replied.

I went over to give my dad a kiss. As I leaned over him he grabbed my arm. "You're a good girl, Kimberly," he whispered into my ear. "Take care of your mother, OK?"

My heart stopped. What did he mean by that? Take care of her *now* or take care of her *forever*? Didn't he think he'd be around to take care of her anymore?

Eight

I yawned and stretched out on the ugly yellow couch in the hospital waiting room. It was almost seven o'clock in the morning, and the sun was coming up. My mother was pacing back and forth, ranting and raving.

"I thought moving back here to Sweet Valley would help with the stress, not make it worse," she said. "Of course, he doesn't watch what he eats. I bet he had a greasy cheeseburger for lunch yesterday. Maybe even two of them.

"And he doesn't get any exercise. He doesn't even walk to get his greasy cheeseburger. He sends his secretary out to get it. She gets all the exercise while he gets all the fat.

"The doctor warned him he had to eat better and get some exercise."

"He did take up a hobby," I said in a small voice.

Mom blinked. "What?" She looked surprised I was even there.

"A hobby," I repeated. "The doctor also told Dad he should take up a hobby and he did do that."

I looked down at the floor. I felt bad about not wanting Dad to do his magic tricks in front of my friends. What's a little embarrassment if doing those tricks was good for Dad's heart?

"Of course." Mom nodded knowingly. "Those magic tricks of his. Well, what good is a hobby if he's going to eat *cheeseburgers* every day?"

I took a deep breath, then stretched my arms above my head. I didn't want to talk about what Dad *should* have done. It wasn't like he could go back and change it now. I wanted to talk about . . . I wasn't sure what I wanted to talk about. I let my arms drop heavily to the couch.

"It's seven o'clock," Mom said abruptly. "Let's go see how he's doing."

"OK," I agreed, standing up. I followed her down the hall to the ICU. When we got there, a heavyset nurse blocked the doorway. "Are you two here to see Paul Haver?" she asked, folding her arms across her large chest.

I felt a chill run up my spine. No one had stopped us at the door before.

Mom moved a stray piece of hair away from her face. "Yes, we are," she said, her eyes widening with alarm. "Is there a problem?"

"No, not at all." The nurse smiled reassuringly. "It's just that he's sleeping right now and I don't think he should be disturbed. He's stable, so maybe this is a good time for you all to get some rest."

I breathed a sigh of relief.

Mom bit her lip. "I don't know," she said, glancing over toward Dad's cubicle. From where we were standing, we could see the foot of his bed, but not his face.

Mom rubbed her hands nervously. "I feel like I should be here," she told the nurse. "In case something happens."

"Well, we've got a room right here on this floor for ICU family members," the nurse informed us. "There are chairs in there that open into cots and I can bring you some bedding. Why don't you two go lie down for a couple of hours? We'll come and get you if there are any changes."

"Well . . . ," Mom said hesitantly. She was having a really hard time making decisions for herself right now.

I remembered what Dad had told me earlier this morning: to take care of Mom. Maybe he meant I should make sure she eats and sleeps, that kind of thing?

I cleared my throat. "I think we should go lie down, Mom," I said in my most grown-up-sounding voice. "Dad's sleeping now anyway. They'll come get us when he wakes up, won't you?" I asked the nurse.

"Sure will," the nurse promised.

Mom sighed heavily. "OK."

"Your husband is scheduled for a second enzyme test around noon, and then depending on how that goes, possibly an angiogram and an echocardiogram later today," the nurse informed us as she led us down the hall.

"And we'll know more once we get the results of those tests?" Mom asked worriedly. Her eyes were red. And there were dark circles under them. She definitely needed some sleep.

The nurse smiled sympathetically. "You'll know whether he's had a heart attack and how bad it was," she confirmed.

"And we'll know whether he's going to be OK?" Mom pressed.

"Only time will tell you that, ma'am," the nurse replied. She opened a door and gestured for us to go inside.

There were four chairs positioned around a glass table. The centerpiece was a basket of plastic yellow flowers.

"All four of these chairs open into beds," the nurse explained. "Just take the cushion off."

She opened a cabinet behind the door. "It looks like there are already sheets in here."

I took the sheets from her. "Thank you," I said politely. "We'll be fine."

"Just let us know when Paul wakes up again, OK?" Mom begged. Her eyes were tearing up again.

"Will do." The nurse smiled, then closed the door on her way out.

Once she was gone, the room was deathly quiet. I could almost hear the sound of my own heart beating. "Um, here are the sheets," I said flatly as I held out the stack of freshly pressed linens.

Mom turned her back to me and walked slowly to the window. I could tell by the way her shoulders heaved that she was crying. We're not a very emotional family, so seeing my mother cry really scared me.

I bit my lip. I didn't know what to do. Part of me wanted to go over to her, but part of me didn't. I was afraid that if I comforted her, I'd probably break down and start crying myself. Which would be almost as bad as crying in front of Dad.

I decided to go make up the beds instead.

Unfortunately it didn't take very long. When I finished, I went over to close the shade. Mom didn't even notice when the shade came down in front of her. I touched her arm. "Mom?" I said softly.

She turned. A single tear ran down her cheek. "Kimberly," she said. Then she grabbed me and hugged me tight.

Her whole body shook. "Oh, Kimberly," she sobbed as she stroked my hair.

I felt my throat tighten, but I didn't give in to the tears. I had to be strong. My parents were counting on me.

Mom finally fell asleep, but I was still wide awake. Once again my body was tired, but my brain wouldn't shut off. I was too worried. Too on edge. I'd kept my feelings inside this whole time and now I felt like I was ready to burst. But I couldn't. At least, not around my mom.

I wished I had an older sister. Someone I could dump on. Someone who could help me be strong. Someone who could help take care of Mom. So all the responsibility didn't fall on me.

If I had a sister, we'd help each other get through this the way my friends and I always helped each other through the rough times.

My friends. It was weird, but the friends that came to mind were the *Unicorns,* not the Eights. I suppose that's natural. The Unicorns have been through a lot together. Ellen's parents' divorce. Mandy's cancer. I hadn't been with the Eights long enough yet to have gone through a crisis with them.

I glanced up at the clock. It was only eight-forty. Julia and the other Eights were at school. They'd probably noticed I wasn't there, though. They'd probably try to call me during lunch, but there wouldn't be any answer at my house.

I'd call Julia at school right now if I thought the teachers would let me talk to her. I was desperate to talk to someone.

I felt my throat closing. I was going to cry.

No, I wasn't!

Get control, Kimberly. Get control.

I glanced up at the clock again. 8:42. In exactly five hours and forty-eight minutes I could call Julia.

I sighed. Five hours and forty-eight minutes was a long time away!

"So where were you today?" Julia asked when I was finally able to call her.

It was almost six o'clock. Dad had had a lot of tests and things earlier, so I hadn't had a chance to get away before. But now here I was, talking to her on a pay phone in the hospital lobby.

There was a gift shop across from the phones, so I had practically no privacy. But I didn't care. It was just so good to hear Julia's voice. So good to finally be able to talk to someone.

"I've been at the hospital," I said, twirling my finger around the heavy metal phone cord.

"The hospital!" Julia screeched. "Why? What's wrong?"

I took a deep breath. "Um, my dad . . . had a heart attack last night."

"Oh. Gee, that's, uh, really too bad, Kimberly." Julia sounded really uncomfortable. Like she didn't know what to say. I couldn't blame her. I didn't really know what to say either.

I leaned my head against the wall. "Yeah, it's been kind of a rough day. It's like . . ." I paused, trying to think of exactly the right words to describe how I was feeling.

"I know what you mean, Kimberly," Julia said right away. "Today was the worst day ever! For me too."

"Really?" I sniffed.

"Yeah," Julia went on. "I totally blew the history test. I just like . . . froze. I mean, I knew all the answers, but I couldn't write them down. It was like my arm was paralyzed. Has that ever happened to you?"

"Um, I don't know. I don't think so."

I knew what Julia was doing. She was trying to make me feel better by trying to make me focus on something besides my dad. She didn't realize that I *wanted* to talk about him.

"Anyway," I said. "My dad had some really scary tests a little while ago. We don't know about the results yet—"

"Oops," Julia interrupted. "Hang on, Kimberly. I've got a call on the other line."

I sighed. I hated call waiting! But I knew Julia had to answer the other call. It might be someone for her parents.

While Julia was gone, I watched people walk in and out of the gift shop. It looked like they sold just about everything in there. Books, cards, balloons, T-shirts.

I watched a man and little girl buy a balloon that said, "It's a Boy!" And I watched an elderly couple buy a card. Was Julia ever going to come back?

Click. "OK, I'm back," Julia announced. "That was Carmen. She says hi."

Carmen? Julia was talking to *Carmen* all that time when she knew I was sitting here in a hospital phone booth waiting for her? Well, I supposed when Julia told Carmen about my dad, she probably had to hear all about it.

"Tell Carmen I said hi," I told Julia.

"OK!" Julia said briskly. "She's still on the other line. Hang on a sec."

"Wait—"

Click.

I bit my lip. What was wrong? Didn't Julia understand I really needed to talk right now? Why did she put me on hold again?

Click.

"Kimberly? Carmen wants to know whether she can get a ride to Fun City from you tonight since you're kind of in her neighborhood?"

My jaw dropped open. *A ride to Fun City?* Had Julia heard a word I said before Carmen called?

"Kimberly? Are you there?"

"Um, yeah," I said weakly. "Listen. My dad's in *intensive care*. I can't go to Fun City tonight."

"Duh! Stupid me!" Julia said. I could almost see her slapping her hand to her head. "You just said that about your dad, didn't you. Hang on. Let me tell Carmen."

"No, wait!" I cried. I did *not* want to be put on hold again.

Surprisingly enough, I didn't hear the click this time. Julia was still there.

"Um, I should probably get back to my mom," I said softly. "So maybe we should just say good-bye."

"Oh," Julia said flatly. "OK. I understand."

"Good," I said as tears filled my eyes.

"I suppose you can't go to the concert tomorrow night either?" Julia remarked.

The concert! I had totally forgotten about the Johnny Buck concert. I wiped my tears on my sleeve. *Be strong,* I reminded myself.

I cleared my throat. "No, probably not," I admitted. At the moment the concert didn't seem very important.

"Well, that's OK," Julia said quickly. "And don't worry about the money for the ticket either. I'm sure we can find *somebody* else who will buy your ticket from us."

I blinked, but it didn't do any good. Tears were running down my cheeks like rivers. Was that all the Eights were concerned about? The concert and rides to Fun City? Didn't they care about me and what I was going through?

Well, front-row seats had to be expensive. And Julia *did* say I shouldn't worry about the money for the ticket. I didn't want to be *too* hard on her.

"I'll see you in school next week," I said finally.

"For sure. Oh, and I hope your dad gets better real soon."

"Thanks," I whispered.

I hung up the phone, but I didn't get up from my bench. I just didn't have the strength.

Nine

On Saturday they moved my dad from intensive care to the coronary care unit down the hall.

The coronary care unit had regular hospital rooms instead of the little glass cubicles all around the nurses' station. Dad still had to wear those circles on his chest, and when he went to the bathroom, he had to drag an IV pole in with him. But other than that he was like a regular patient now. He was even wearing his own pajamas from home.

He could also have flowers, so Mom and I chose a bouquet of daisies and carnations from the gift shop downstairs. We could visit anytime we wanted and stay as long as we wanted.

Around one o'clock the doctor came to check on Dad. She was young, with long dark curly hair. She looked young for a doctor, but her name tag read "Dr. Weydert."

"You've had a heart attack, Mr. Haver," Dr. Weydert said in a serious voice as she opened a manila folder and took out some papers.

I swallowed hard. Mom reached for my hand. "It definitely was a heart attack?" she asked with concern.

"Yes," Dr. Weydert replied crisply. She took a colorful diagram out of the folder to show us. "Here you can see the different parts of the heart and how the blood flows in and out," she said, pointing to the red veins and blue arteries. "You were very lucky, Mr. Haver. You had a mild heart attack—"

"Mild?" I repeated. My dad was in so much pain that he couldn't move and that was a *mild* heart attack?

The doctor paused. "Well, the heart attack caused just slight damage—"

"How slight?" Mom interrupted.

Dr. Weydert scratched her head. "Maybe about ten percent damage to the left ventricle. And if you're going to have a heart attack, the left ventricle is the place to have it," she said cheerfully. "The rest of the heart will compensate for a weakness in the left ventricle."

"In other words, it wasn't much of a heart attack at all," Dad said in a voice that sounded almost cheerful. He was sitting up in bed, propped up by some pillows. He looked weak, but he didn't seem to be in any pain.

"That doesn't mean you should take this lightly." Mom frowned at Dad. "It was *still* a heart attack."

"Your wife is right, Mr. Haver," Dr. Weydert warned. She held up her chart again and pointed to one of the arteries. "Your angiogram showed a fifty to seventy-five percent blockage right about here. Now you're not going to need angioplasty. We've got medication to treat that blockage. But you will have to make some lifestyle changes."

"That means no more greasy fast food!" Mom said firmly.

"No, it means no more greasy fast food *in front of you*," Dad teased. Then he winked at me.

The doctor pursed her lips.

Mom shook her head. But I grinned in spite of myself. Even though a lot of what the doctor said sounded pretty serious, it was good to see Dad goofing around. It made this whole thing seem a little less scary.

By late Saturday afternoon I was exhausted. Mom and I were sitting in the lounge down the hall from Dad's room. Several of his friends from work had stopped in, bringing flowers and cards. Mom thought we should leave for a while so the room wasn't too crowded.

"Why don't you go on home, Kimberly, and get some rest," Mom suggested, rubbing the bridge of her nose.

"If I do go home, will you come too?" I asked meekly.

"Not yet." She shook her head. "If your father is doing OK, I may come home to sleep tonight. But for now I'm going to stay. They're going to let him get up in a while and take a walk down the hallway. I'd like to be here for that."

I nodded. Part of me wanted to stay too. But I was so exhausted that another part of me wanted to go home. I just didn't want to go home *alone*. "I'll stay too," I declared.

Mom smiled. "All right, honey. Why don't you and I go down to the cafeteria and grab a bite to eat. Maybe when we get back, your father will be ready to get up."

"OK," I said, dragging myself up from my chair. My throat felt raw from swallowing my tears all day long. I was so tired that each step I took was painful. But somehow I managed to follow my mother out of the lounge.

Now that Dad seemed to be doing better, Mom had perked up a bit. At least she was thinking about things like food and sleep again.

You'd think all that would make me feel better too. But it didn't. I was just so tired. And scared. And lonely.

What if my dad had another heart attack? That's what happened to Grandpa Haver. He had a heart attack and everyone thought he was better. But then he had another heart attack and *died*.

"Are you doing OK, honey?" Mom asked as we waited for the elevator to arrive.

But before I could answer, the elevator bell rang and the doors opened. Out stepped our neighbor, Mrs. Greenfield. "Barbara!" she cried as soon as she saw us.

"Hi, Joni," Mom responded. Mrs. Greenfield wrapped her arms around Mom first. Then she gave my shoulders a squeeze.

Mrs. Greenfield had about a million questions about Dad, so she and my mom sat down on the bench outside the elevator. Mom started at the beginning and told Mrs. Greenfield everything that had happened in the last two days. Mrs. Greenfield listened quietly and patted Mom's arm sympathetically.

My stomach knotted as I watched them. I know it was selfish of me, but I couldn't help feeling jealous. Mom's friend came to see her, but none of my friends had come to see me.

I didn't expect the Unicorns to come. I had never called them and told them I was here. But I *did* call Julia. Didn't she care about how I was handling this?

I wandered over to the window. Maybe Julia and the others were on their way to see me? Maybe they were out front right now?

I looked down over the parking lot. But the only people I saw were two nurses who were leaving the hospital and an elderly man who was coming in.

I sighed. It was almost dinnertime and not one of the Eights had called me or come to see me all day. Of course, they were busy getting ready for the Johnny Buck concert tonight, but wouldn't you think one of them could have taken a few minutes to give me a call? Just to let me know they'd been thinking about me.

But maybe the Eights *had* tried. Maybe you couldn't come up to the coronary care unit unless you were sixteen or something. Maybe if I went downstairs, there would be a message for me at the front desk.

I pushed the elevator button. "I'm going to go downstairs for a while," I told my mother when the door opened.

She glanced up. "I'll meet you in the cafeteria in a few minutes," she replied.

"OK," I said. The elevator doors closed.

When they opened again, I was back in the lobby. My heart leaped when I saw a girl about my age. She had her back to me, but I would've known that curtain of red hair anywhere.

"Marcy!" I called, running over to the girl.

But when the girl turned, I felt a hollow emptiness in the pit of my stomach. It wasn't Marcy. It wasn't anybody I knew at all.

"Sorry," I muttered. "I thought you were someone else."

I wandered over to the receptionist. "Excuse me. Do you have any messages for Kimberly Haver?" I asked hopefully.

The woman tucked a few strands of her gray hair behind her ear and glanced down at some papers in front of her. "Haver?" she asked. "No, I'm sorry. I don't have anything for anyone by that name."

I sighed. "Thanks anyway."

"Mom?" I asked, pulling the crust off one of my sandwich halves. We were having a light dinner in the hospital cafeteria. "How old do you have to be to visit in the coronary care unit?"

Mom dabbed the corners of her mouth with her napkin. "I don't know; twelve or thirteen. But you don't have to worry, Kimberly. If you weren't allowed to visit your dad, someone would've told us by now."

"I wasn't talking about me," I said glumly. Then I stopped. I shouldn't burden Mom with my problems. At least not now.

"It was nice of Mrs. Greenfield to stop by," I said,

popping a piece of bread crust into my mouth.

"Yes, it was," Mom agreed. "She's a good friend."

There was that stab of jealousy again. I glanced up at the clock on the wall behind my mom. It was six-thirty. The Eights would be leaving for the concert any minute. There was no way they'd stop by now.

Mom set down her napkin and suddenly reached for my arm. "I don't know what's been going on between you and your friends, Kimberly," Mom said. "But you should realize that some people have a very hard time offering support at a time like this."

I bit my lip and nodded grimly.

"Hospitals make people uncomfortable," Mom went on. "I think friends who are willing to come to the hospital to offer support are really special friends."

I felt a knot in my stomach. I guess that meant I didn't have any special friends, I thought as tears sprang to my eyes. But I blinked them away. I didn't want my mother to know how upset I was. She had enough to worry about.

"Kimberly?" came a tentative voice behind me.

My heart stopped. They *did* come! I knew they would. They wouldn't go to the concert without stopping by to see me for a few minutes.

I whirled around. "Hi, you guys—" My jaw just about dropped to the floor. It wasn't Julia and the Eights who were there. It was the Unicorns.

They were wearing their purple T-shirts that spelled out, "We Love Johnny Buck." Except the way they were standing, it read "Johnny Love Buck We."

"What . . . what are you guys doing here?" I asked.

Ellen pulled up a chair beside me. "We just heard," she said sympathetically.

Lila sat down on the other side of me. "We were at Bruce's party and someone asked where you were. Julia said your dad had a *heart attack!*"

"Is he going to be OK?" Jessica asked with concern.

"I think I'll head back upstairs," Mom interrupted. "You stay and chat with your friends as long as you like."

Mandy sucked her purple bubble back into her mouth. "We're really sorry to hear about Mr. Haver," she told Mom.

"Thank you, dear." Mom smiled at Mandy. "But he's going to be just fine."

Once Mom was gone, the Unicorns all turned to me. "So what happened?" Lila asked.

"Uh, well," I said, wiping my hands on my jeans. I felt really uncomfortable. I wasn't sure why the Unicorns had come, so I wasn't sure just how much I should say. "Well, my dad had a mild heart attack. The doctor said that if you're going to have a heart attack, my dad had it in the best place."

"That's good!" Jessica said with relief. "I guess."

"So he's really going to be OK?" Lila asked nervously.

"We think so," I replied.

Mandy reached for my hand. "What about you?" she asked, looking deep into my eyes. "Are *you* OK?"

I felt a catch in my throat. After all that had happened between us this week, I didn't feel I could let them know how I was really feeling. So I swallowed my tears. "Sure," I said breezily. "I'm fine."

But I didn't *feel* fine. I didn't feel fine at all.

Jessica glanced at Lila. "Well, we just wanted to make sure you were OK," she said, standing up.

They were *leaving*? Already?

"I'm sorry we can't stay longer," Lila apologized. "But Daddy's waiting in the limo downstairs."

"Can you believe it?" Ellen snorted. "Lila's *dad* is going to the concert with us."

"He's keeping his promise about spending more time with me," Lila said. "Of course I never expected him to come with me and my friends to a rock concert."

I forced a smile. "That's great," I said, feeling my lip quiver. I blinked back my tears. I had no right to expect the Unicorns to stay with me. Especially after the way I'd treated them all week.

But the thought of them leaving, the thought of being alone again, tore me up inside.

Jessica touched my shoulder. "We know you're an Eight now," she said in an understanding voice. "But we've been friends for a long time, Kimberly. We just wanted you to know that we still care about you."

I nodded. I felt the same way about them.

"And we still want to be friends even if you're not in the club anymore," Mandy added.

My whole body was shaking because I was trying so hard not to cry. *Get it together*, I told myself. The last thing I wanted to do was make the Unicorns think I wasn't in complete control.

"We should probably go," Lila said softly.

"Yeah, by the time we get to the Amphitheater, the concert will probably be starting," Mandy agreed.

I pressed my lips together, but I couldn't hold the tears back any longer. "Do you guys *have* to go?" I blurted.

Jessica's eyebrows jumped. Mandy looked at me in shock.

Tears poured down my face. I put my hand up to my mouth, closed my eyes, and just let the tears flow. I must have looked so pathetic.

Ellen put an arm around me. Lila took my hand. And Jessica stroked my arm.

"We'll stay if you really want us to," Mandy said soothingly.

"P-P-Please!" I choked. "Please stay!"

Ten

It wasn't until I was lying in my own bed on Sunday night that it hit me. *The Unicorns had given up going to the Johnny Buck concert for me*. The Unicorns had given up the concert while the Eights had never come to see me at all.

Mom said it was hard for some people to come to a hospital to offer support. But the Eights hadn't even called and left a message on our answering machine.

Didn't they care about me at all? Didn't they think I was really one of them?

Dad was doing fine. Mom and I spent the day watching videotapes on nutrition and exercise with him. He even asked Mom to bring in his magic set so he could show off to the nurses.

Now that Dad was doing better, I'd be going

back to school. But I was confused. I wasn't sure who my friends were.

Jessica said she and the Unicorns still cared about me, but I was an Eight now.

Was I an Eight?

I had to admit, I enjoyed hanging out with Julia and the others. They were fun and sophisticated and they were friends with high-school boys. But they had let me down. When it really mattered, they weren't there for me.

The Unicorns were there for me, but they were still the same old Unicorns. Mandy still cracked her gum and blew bubbles all over her face. Ellen still wore her hair like a second-grader. And I doubted Jessica had given up making prank phone calls. They hadn't grown up at all in the last week. But I had. My dad's heart attack forced me to grow up even more.

In fact, that difference in maturity between me and the Unicorns was probably bigger than ever now.

"Kimberly! You're back!" Julia said. It was noon Monday and she had just come up behind me in the lunch line.

"Hi, Julia," I responded, helping myself to a cup of yogurt. She looked happy to see me.

See, I told myself. *They care about you.* It was like Mom said. They just were uncomfortable coming to the hospital. Especially when they'd really only known me a week.

"I know Greg's going to be really happy to see you," Julia prattled on. "He was asking about you this weekend."

My heart gave a stir at the mention of Greg's name.

Julia grabbed a bottle of mineral water. "You'll be able to come to Fun City after school, won't you?" she asked.

"Maybe for a little while," I agreed. "I'll want to get to the hospital by four o'clock, though."

I followed Julia over to the Eights' table. Along the way we passed the Unicorner.

"Hi, Kimberly," Mandy called, waving to me.

I stopped. "Hi," I said shyly. Julia glanced back at me and frowned. Then she kept right on walking.

"How's your dad?" Ellen's forehead wrinkled with concern.

"Oh, fine," I replied cheerfully. "He's probably going to come home the end of the week."

I wondered whether the Unicorns would invite me to eat with them. Suddenly I felt choked with longing. I probably *would* eat with them. If they asked me to. I mean, they gave up the Johnny Buck concert to sit with me at the hospital on Saturday night. The least I could do was eat one lousy lunch with them.

Lila grinned. "That's good."

"Say hi to him for us," Jessica said.

Then they all turned back to their discussion. They obviously didn't *want* me to eat with them.

I felt a cold fist close over my heart. I definitely wasn't a Unicorn anymore.

"Wow, you look great, Kimberly!" Susan gushed as I set my tray down beside hers and sat down.

I raised my eyebrows. I looked *great?* I knew for a fact there were bags under my eyes from the lack of sleep this weekend.

"Yeah, that's a really cool blouse," Kristin complimented me. "Where did you get it?"

I looked down at my plain white blouse. It wasn't anything special. "I think it was a gift," I said.

I waited for someone to ask about my dad. But no one did. Maybe they needed a little nudge. Some reminder of the past weekend. "So did you guys have fun at the concert?" I asked, opening my milk carton.

Seven faces gaped at me. "You mean you haven't heard?" Marcy asked incredulously.

"Heard what?" Did Johnny Buck pull one of them up onstage or something?

"There was no concert Saturday night," Marcy said soberly.

"There wasn't? Why not?" I wanted to know.

"Johnny was warming up backstage and all of a sudden, his voice just gave out," Carmen informed me.

"Really?" I wasn't really thinking about Johnny Buck. I was thinking only one terrible thing—the concert was canceled and *still* none of the Eights came to see me in the hospital.

"Yeah. He's going to do another concert next weekend to make up for it," Gretchen put in.

"Wow," I said, surprised.

"You'll be able to go, won't you?" Marcy asked me.

"Well," I said carefully. "It depends on when my dad gets out of the hospital. If the concert is the same day my dad comes home, I don't know if I'll want to go."

Julia glanced at Carmen, who shifted uncomfortably.

"I guess we'll just play it by ear, then," Susan said, poking at her salad.

"Fine," I said, swallowing my disappointment.

Nobody seemed to know what to say after that. The Eights concentrated on their salads and I poked at my pizza. I knew they were uncomfortable, but couldn't they say *something* about my dad? "Hey, did you guys notice what Mandy Miller is wearing today?" Kristin asked, changing the subject.

Everyone turned around to look. Mandy was wearing a pair of men's yellow and green plaid trousers with a white shirt and a funky yellow tie.

"What, does she buy all her clothes at the Salvation Army?" Erica asked with a sneer.

My back stiffened. "Most of them," I admitted.

The Eights all burst out laughing.

"Aw, isn't that a shame," Gretchen said sarcastically. "Poor little Mandy can't afford new clothes."

I stared at Gretchen. I might not be a Unicorn anymore, but that didn't mean I wanted to listen to the Eights trash them all the time. "I don't think it's a matter of not being able to afford new clothes," I spoke up. But I knew perfectly well Mandy's family wasn't exactly rich. "She just likes thrift store stuff."

"Yeah, well, there's no accounting for taste, is there?" Julia said, giggling. "I mean, look who she hangs out with!"

I swallowed hard. Until a week ago *I* was one of the people Mandy hung out with.

"Really!" Marcy added, rolling her eyes. "The Unicorns are so lame."

That did it. "The *Unicorns* are lame?" I exploded, slamming my pizza down. I let out a short laugh. "Who are you guys to judge the Unicorns?"

Susan and Gretchen's mouths dropped open.

Julia and Carmen exchanged a look.

"No, really!" I said. Now that I'd started, I couldn't stop. I'd held it in too long. "You guys call yourselves friends. But what kind of friends are you? You're there for the good times. But what about the bad times? Where are you then?"

Kristin sighed heavily.

Erica looked bored.

"You're off at some stupid Johnny Buck concert!" I spat out.

The Eights all looked confused.

"Excuse me, Kimberly," Gretchen said, blinking. "But we already told you. There was no concert last Saturday."

"Yeah," Marcy chimed in. "And even if he did have a concert, it certainly wouldn't be *stupid!*" She folded her arms across her chest and glanced around the table like *I* was being stupid.

"That's not the point!" I cried, throwing up my hands.

"Just what *is* the point, Kimberly?" Julia asked impatiently.

My eyes filled with tears. "The point is the Unicorns were there for me last weekend when I needed friends. And you guys weren't." I lowered my eyes.

I figured they'd apologize. I figured they'd think about what I said and it would hit them that I was right. And they'd feel really bad and beg for my forgiveness.

But it wasn't anything like that.

"Well, if you still think the Unicorns are so great, maybe you'd rather go back to them," Carmen said in a low voice.

"Maybe I would," I said, shoving my chair back from the table. I stood up. "At least they know what true friendship is all about!"

"Oh, and we don't?" Carmen snorted.

I shook my head as a single tear trickled down my cheek. But I didn't bother to wipe it away. "You don't have a clue," I said, narrowing my eyes at all seven of them.

Then I took off for the bathroom before the entire school saw me crying.

I was such an idiot. I had blown it with the Unicorns. I had blown it with the Eights. And now the thing I feared most had happened. I had absolutely no friends.

I had locked myself in a stall in an upstairs bathroom. The bathroom that was farthest away from the Eights' office. Not that I expected them to come looking for me. Not that I even *wanted* them to come looking for me.

As I tore off a few squares of toilet paper and blew my nose I heard someone enter the bathroom. I pulled up my feet and straddled the toilet. Who was out there?

"Is she in here?" someone whispered.

"I don't know," someone else whispered back. It sounded like Jessica.

I peered through the crack in the door. It *was* Jessica. And all the other Unicorns too.

"Kimberly?" Mandy asked out loud.

I was stunned. What were they doing here? After the way I'd treated them, why would they come looking for me?

Someone pounded on my door. "Kimberly?" Jessica wondered. "Is that you in there?"

"Yeah," I squeaked, wiping my hand across my eyes.

"Are you coming out?" Lila wanted to know.

I sniffed. "I don't think so," I said sadly. I couldn't face them. I was too ashamed. How could I have thought the Eights' friendship was as real as the Unicorns'?

"We, uh, heard you quit the Eights," Ellen said tentatively, stepping up to the door.

I could tell they were all clustered around my stall. I saw Mandy's combat boots. Lila's blue flats. Ellen's oxfords. And Jessica's loafers.

I sniffed again. "I, uh, never officially joined the Eights," I told them.

"You didn't?" Lila asked.

"No," I admitted, hugging my elbows. "They wanted me to, but it just never felt totally right. And now . . ." I glanced up at the ceiling. "I don't know. It just feels totally wrong."

"That's because it *is* wrong!" Jessica said firmly.

"You belong with us, Kimberly," Lila informed me.

I peered out through the crack. "With you?" I was amazed. "You mean you still want me to be a Unicorn?"

"If you want to be," Mandy replied with uncertainty.

I unlatched the door and slowly opened it. As soon as I did Ellen stepped forward and threw her arms around me. Mandy, Jessica, and Lila all crowded in too. And pretty soon I was bawling again. Suddenly it hit me. How could I have thought the Unicorns were immature? So what if they acted a little silly sometimes? They were way more mature than the Eights in ways that really mattered—and they were the best friends I'd ever had in my life.

We hugged for a long time. Then I went to get some more toilet paper. I broke off a few squares for myself, then passed the rest to Mandy.

Mandy tore off a section of toilet paper and passed it to Ellen.

"What I don't understand is why you even started hanging out with the Eights to begin with," Mandy said, but she didn't sound accusing.

"Yeah, the Eights are our *enemies!*" Jessica blurted.

Lila looked at her. "*Enemies* is a pretty strong word," she said diplomatically.

Ellen sniffed. "We've just never gotten along with them," she said weakly. "We couldn't believe it when you started hanging out with them."

I lowered my head. "I know," I said, ashamed. "And I'm sorry. But you guys have to understand something. You guys are seventh-graders. I'm an *eighth*-grader."

Jessica looked at me blankly. "So?"

"So sometimes it's *hard* being the only eighth-grader," I explained. "I mean next year I'm going to go off to high school all by myself. You guys will still be here. What am I supposed to do then?"

Mandy shrugged. "The same thing Janet and Tamara and Grace did."

"But they're not even friends anymore. That's sort of why I started hanging out with the Eights," I tried to explain. "I wanted to have someone to hang out with in high school."

"But Kimberly, you'll make *new* friends in high school," Mandy said, cracking her gum.

Lila tossed her hair over her shoulder. "Yeah," she agreed. "I don't think Janet, Tamara, and Grace hate each other or anything. They probably just don't have any classes together."

"And they're probably all in different after-school activities," Jessica pointed out.

"Probably." Lila nodded.

That was exactly what Tamara had said the other day.

"They've all made tons of new friends," Lila went on. "You will too, Kimberly."

"Plus you'll still have us," Mandy promised.

"Yeah, you can hang out with us anytime you want," Jessica said, grinning. "You can introduce us to all your high-school friends."

"Especially the cute guys," Ellen put in.

I thought about the Eights and the high-school kids they hung out with at Fun City. Maybe by next year the Unicorns would have a place like Fun City to hang out at. And maybe I *would* come back and bring some of my high-school friends with me. That would be pretty cool.

Until then, I still had the rest of this year to enjoy being a Unicorn.

Eleven

Dad was looking pretty good on Wednesday after school. The heart monitor had been taken off and he was sitting up in bed with what looked like a brand-new magic trick in his hands.

"Kimberly!" He smiled when he noticed me standing in the doorway. "Come on in."

I went in and sat down at the foot of his bed. "What's that?" I asked, nodding at the funny sticks he was holding in a V in his hand. They looked like drumsticks with red tassels on the ends. As he pulled one tassel down, the other tassel went up.

"Chinese magic sticks," Dad replied.

"*Magic* sticks, huh?" I said in a teasing voice.

"Yup." Dad nodded as he continued to pull the tassels. "Notice how when I pull this tassel down, the other one goes up."

"Amazing," I said, clasping my hands to my cheeks. This time I wasn't going to give Dad a hard time about his hobby. The doctor said having a hobby was good for Dad's heart. So fine. I'd play along.

Dad cocked his head. "You don't look very impressed, Kimberly," he said cheerfully, still pulling on the tassels. "What's the matter? Don't you believe these sticks are really magic?"

"Well . . ." I hesitated. I mean, I could tell the sticks were connected somehow in back. But because of the way Dad was holding them, you couldn't actually see *how* they were connected.

"Well what?" Dad pressed as he continued to pull on the tassels. He slapped his palm to his head. "Oh, I get it. I bet you think these sticks are connected, don't you?"

"Aren't they?" I asked, raising an eyebrow.

Dad shook his head as he slowly opened his fist and held the sticks parallel to each other. Once again he pulled one tassel down and the other went up. Down and up. Down and up. How did he do that if they weren't connected?

"Hey, that's pretty good," I said enthusiastically.

"Thank you," Dad replied, taking a bow. Then he pulled one tassel down and the other one *didn't* go back up.

His face fell. "Uh-oh," he said in a worried voice. "What happened?"

He held the sticks right where they were and referred to an instruction sheet in his lap. "Hmmm, doesn't say anything about that happening in here," he muttered.

I swallowed hard. Dad looked *so* disappointed. He pulled on one tassel, then the other. But nothing happened. They both hung limply from the sticks.

"D-D-Did you break them?" I asked nervously as I leaned over and tried to read his instruction sheet.

Dad pulled the instruction sheet away. "No, I don't think so," he replied. "Why don't you try waving your hands over them while I say a few magic words."

"Oh, is this still part of the trick?" I asked, scratching my head.

Dad shrugged. "Just try it. We'll see what happens."

"OK," I said. I waved my hands over the sticks.

"Abracadabra alacazam!" Dad exclaimed.

Right before my eyes both tassels disappeared into the sticks.

I gaped. "How did you do that?"

"Ancient Chinese secret," Dad said modestly. He pulled one tassel down. Then he pulled the other tassel down and the first tassel went up. Down and up. Down and up. "Looks like they still work," he said, sighing with relief. "Your mom just gave me these this morning. She would've been upset if she thought I'd broken them already."

I frowned. "Come on, Dad. Show me how you did that."

He handed me the sticks. They were surprisingly heavy. Especially on the top where the tassels were. They tipped forward and both tassels spilled down.

I automatically pulled the sticks up and both tassels went up. Just like they had for Dad.

"Hey, I get it," I said grinning. "There's a little magnet or something at the top. So when you hold the sticks up a little, the tassels come up. *Both* of them come up. Unless you're holding one down."

I experimented to see if I was right. I pulled both tassels down and raised the sticks, and both tassels went right back up. "Cool!"

"Yeah," Dad said, looking thoughtful. "It *is* cool."

I gave the sticks back to Dad. "You can't tell there's something weird about these things just by looking at them," I said.

"That's what I like about magic," Dad said in a serious voice. "Things are seldom as they appear at first glance. You have to examine something from all angles and then the solution seems very simple."

Things are seldom as they appear at first glance. Boy, that was sure true about the Eights. They seemed like such a close-knit group of friends when I first got to know them. I thought they really cared about me. But they cared a lot more about having fun.

I can have *fun* with just about anybody. When it comes to choosing a club, I want a club that's really going to be there for me.

"They're always there, they pick you up, they show you that they care. . . ."

I wasn't the sort of person who paid a lot of attention to song lyrics. If the song had a good beat or a nice tune, I liked it. Most of the time I didn't even know what the song was about.

But on Wednesday night, when I was doing my homework to Johnny Buck's latest CD, the words caught my attention.

"They're the friends that last forever, the friends that you remember, the friends you made when you were small; they're there no matter what. . . ."

I put my pencil down and just listened closely to the rest of the song. By the time it was over, there were tears streaming down my face.

I wiped them away. I don't know what it was these last couple of days, but it seemed like I was constantly crying.

The next track on the CD was "Come on Down," which had a much faster beat. Don't ask me what it was about.

I got up and switched my player back to "Friends." I just had to hear it again.

"They're there if you should need them, no matter what you've done. . . ."

That line really reminded me of the Unicorns. It was almost like Johnny Buck wrote the song about them. About them being there for me this past weekend, even after I betrayed them.

I sat back down on my bed. Suddenly I had an idea. I could write Johnny Buck a letter. I could tell him about the Unicorns and how they're the kind of friends he sings about in his song. Maybe Johnny would write back and send the Unicorns an autographed picture. Wouldn't that be cool?

I turned the page in my math notebook and began my letter.

"Dear Johnny Buck, I think your song 'Friends' is the best song you ever wrote. Do you have friends like the ones in the song? I do. Let me tell you about them. . . ."

"We brought you something, Kimberly," Mandy said with a grin as she held a medium-size package out to me. She was wearing baggy white pants with her purple "Love" shirt.

Jessica was wearing "We." Lila was wearing "Johnny." Ellen was wearing "Buck." And I was wearing my best jeans with a white blouse.

Since my dad just got out of the hospital

today, we decided to get ready for the Johnny Buck concert at my house.

I took the present from Mandy. "What is it?" I asked, staring at the purple wrapping paper.

"Open it!" the Unicorns said in unison. They all gathered around as I tore off the paper. But for some reason they all seemed a little nervous.

Mandy grabbed the bow and stuck it on Ellen's nose. Ellen giggled. She took the bow and set it on top of Jessica's head. Jessica reached out to put it on *my* head, but then she stopped herself and tossed it in my trash can instead.

I opened the box. Inside was a purple T-shirt just like the ones the other Unicorns were wearing. It was my "You" shirt!

"We, uh, took a chance on you deciding to join us at the concert after all," Ellen said, scrunching up her face.

They all stared at me like they were afraid of my reaction. But for some reason, wearing a message across all our shirts didn't seem as stupid today as it did a couple of weeks ago. In fact, it almost seemed fun!

"I'm glad you did," I said, smiling brightly. "Thanks, you guys." I took off my white blouse and put on the T-shirt instead.

"Let's hope Johnny doesn't get another attack of laryngitis," Jessica said, flipping her hair behind her shoulders.

"Yeah," Ellen chimed in. "He goes on tour around the country next week, so he wouldn't be able to postpone this concert again."

"Relax, you guys," Lila said knowingly. "I'm sure Johnny's been on some sort of antibiotic all week."

Ellen breathed a sigh of relief as she went to my mirror and combed her hair.

"You don't need the whole mirror, do you, Ellen?" Jessica said, nudging her with her hip. She nudged Ellen right into Mandy, who nudged her back into Jessica.

Lila rolled her eyes. "Real mature, guys."

Everyone stopped and looked at me. "What?" I asked. "Why are you all staring at me?"

Then I remembered. This was how the trouble had started—with me thinking the Unicorns were immature.

To show them I was through being an old grouch, I went over to Lila and nudged her into Jessica.

"Hey!" Lila yelled, scrambling to keep her balance on her two-inch heels.

Jessica and Mandy giggled. Pretty soon we were all giggling. The tension was broken.

I watched us in the mirror. You, Johnny, We, Buck, Love was the order we were standing in. We were five best friends, pushing each other and giggling like third-graders. But who cared? I, for one, was having the time of my life.

*   *   *

"Well, look at you! Don't you look nice!" Dad whistled as we entered the living room. He was sitting in his recliner, watching TV.

"Are you girls ready to go?" Mom asked, getting up from the couch. She had promised to drive us all to the concert in our minivan.

"Thanks, Dad," I said, smoothing my T-shirt. I turned to Mom. "I think we're ready."

"Wait a minute!" Dad cried. He reached over and grabbed the deck of cards from the end table beside him. "Before you go, there's this new trick I've been working on."

I groaned. "Not now, Dad. We don't want to be late."

"It won't take very long. Please, one of you come over here and pick a card," Dad pleaded.

"OK. I will," Mandy said, stepping forward. She picked a card.

I sighed. Leave it to Mandy to humor him.

"Show the others your card, then put it back in the deck," Dad instructed.

Mandy turned around and wiggled her eyebrows as she showed us her card. Four of spades.

Ellen giggled.

Mandy returned the card to the deck and waited while Dad shuffled the cards. He fanned the deck face out. "Hmmm," he said, frowning as he stared at the cards. "I don't see your card here."

Mandy leaned over the cards. "I don't see it either," she said in a surprised voice.

Dad scratched his head. "I guess I did something wrong. The idea was to find your card, not make it *disappear*." He went through the cards one by one. "Are you sure it's not in here?" he asked Mandy.

She shook her head. "Sorry, Mr. Haver," she said, grinning. "I don't see it."

Dad shrugged. "Oh, well," he said flippantly. "I guess I still need some practice." He reached into his pants pocket and pulled out his billfold. "Come over here, Kimberly. I want to give you a little something so you can buy me a souvenir at the concert."

"What would you like?" I asked in a teasing voice. "An I-love-Johnny poster?"

As he opened his billfold a playing card fell out. I bent down to pick it up. It was the four of spades!

"Wow!" Ellen exclaimed, wide-eyed.

"That was great, Mr. Haver!" Mandy grinned.

"He's been practicing that trick all day," Mom said proudly.

"I believe it," Lila said, obviously impressed. "You've really gotten good at this magic stuff."

Dad cocked his head. "Better than the last time you were here and I accidentally doused you with milk, huh?"

Lila looked confused. "You never doused me with milk, Mr. Haver."

"Um, Dad? That wasn't Lila. That was Julia and Marcy," I said in a low voice. The last thing I needed was to remind the Unicorns about how I was hanging out with the Eights last week.

But Jessica grinned. "You poured milk on the Eights?" she squealed.

Dad shrugged. "I didn't mean to. I didn't quite have that trick down yet."

The Unicorns all laughed.

"I bet they were really mad," Ellen said with a smile.

"They didn't exactly stick around until Dad got it right," I admitted.

"Aw, that's OK, Mr. Haver," Mandy said, patting his shoulder. "We wouldn't mind if you goofed up and accidentally poured milk on us."

"Yeah, right," I said.

"We wouldn't!" Jessica insisted. Then she turned to my dad and smiled. "We're the *nice* club."

Well, she was right about that anyway.

Twelve

"What time is it?" Ellen asked.

Mandy sighed heavily. "It's about thirty seconds after the last time you asked." She bent her arm so Ellen could read her watch.

We were in our seats at the Sweet Valley Amphitheater, waiting for the Johnny Buck concert to begin. We were all pretty excited.

"Hey, look!" Jessica pointed. "It's the Crazy Eights!"

I turned. The Eights were just now coming up the aisle, waving at people they knew along the way. The concert was supposed to start in five minutes. It was like they got here late so they could make an entrance. They wanted to show everyone *they* had front-row seats.

When they reached our aisle, they stopped. "Well,

look at the Unicorn Club," Carmen said in a snotty voice. "They love Johnny Buck. Aren't they cute?"

Marcy rolled her eyes. "Like Johnny's even going to notice them."

"Oh, I bet he will notice us," I said confidently as I held my purse tighter. I had a little surprise for the Unicorns. *And* for the Eights too, for that matter. I was dying to tell them about it, but I knew it would be better if I waited. Then it would be a *real* surprise.

"Yeah, right," Julia scoffed as she and the other Eights moved on.

I hadn't really spoken to any of them since our big blowup in the cafeteria on Monday. I still saw them in history class, of course. But they just ignored me. It was like the week I had hung out with them had never even happened.

"Do you wish you were sitting in the front row with them?" Lila whispered to me.

Before I could answer her, I noticed Greg, the guy I'd sort of been hanging out with at Fun City. He was sitting in the front row with his arm around Gretchen. I wondered what the Eights told him about me. Why I didn't hang around with them anymore. Maybe he didn't even notice I was gone. Gretchen has the same color hair that I do. For all the attention he ever paid me, maybe he thought I was Gretchen?

I turned to Lila. "I'd rather sit in the balcony

with you guys than the front row with them," I said honestly.

She smiled. "Good."

The lights blinked on and off a couple of times.

"Oh!" Ellen squealed. "It's starting!"

Mandy blew a huge bubble, which popped all over her face. "Oops." She giggled.

I just shook my head as I settled back to enjoy the show with my friends. It was good to be back.

"I'm going to do one more song, then we'll take about a ten-minute break," Johnny Buck announced to the crowd.

We all screamed in response. There was a spotlight on Johnny. And several thousand little flashlights glowed all around the Amphitheater. But the rest of the auditorium was dark.

It was light enough that I could see the Eights leaning on the stage, though. They hadn't been in their chairs once during the whole first part of the show. They pounded on the stage and reached out for Johnny's legs every time he came close to the edge of the stage. Talk about immature!

"I received a letter from one of you this week," Johnny said in a serious voice.

The crowd grew quiet.

"A letter that touched me like no other fan letter has ever touched me before," Johnny went on.

I shivered. This was it! My big surprise.

"The person who wrote this letter told me that my song 'Friends' has special meaning for her because of this great club she's in."

"It can't be any better than our club," Jessica muttered.

I grinned. *Just wait, Jessica,* I thought. *Just wait.*

"This sounds like quite a group," Johnny went on. He took a piece of paper out of his back pocket and unfolded it. "Listen to this. 'I haven't been a very good friend to them lately. But when something happened and I really needed a friend, they were there. It was like they didn't care how badly I had treated them. They knew I needed them.'" Johnny rubbed his face. "Man," he said with awe. "Those are the kinds of friends I'd like to have!"

I could see the Eights exchanging glances, like they were trying to figure out which one of them could have written the letter. But of course none of them had.

Johnny slipped his guitar back over his head. "This one goes out to the Unicorn Club," he said, strumming the opening bars of his song "Friends."

"The Unicorn Club?" Lila gasped.

"Us?" Jessica asked, wide-eyed.

I shrugged modestly. "Unless there's another Unicorn Club around here."

"Did you write that letter, Kimberly?" Ellen leaned forward to ask me.

"Oh, don't make a big deal about it," I said

with a dismissive wave of my hand. The last thing I needed was to start bawling again here in the middle of the concert.

"I, uh, just wanted to thank you guys. You know, for being there for me last week," I explained. I wasn't exactly comfortable talking about my feelings like this, but I did want the Unicorns to know I appreciated them.

"We get the picture," Mandy said dreamily. She was leaning back in her seat, gazing up at Johnny Buck.

The Eights were shooting us dagger looks from the front row. They were finally sitting down. Johnny Buck had noticed *us*, not them.

"They're always there, they pick you up, they show you that they care," Johnny sang.

"Oh, but there's more," I said, unzipping my purse. I pulled out an envelope and the Unicorns crowded in to see what it was. "Johnny Buck's manager called me yesterday after he had read my letter. He said Johnny was so touched that he just had to meet the girls that had inspired me to write to him. So he delivered these." I held up five backstage passes.

"Oh, my gosh!" Jessica clapped her hands to her cheeks. "Are those what I think they are?"

I nodded. "Backstage passes."

Mandy threw her arms around me.

"Kimberly, you're the best!" she yelled in my ear.

"I know," I said modestly.

"Hi, you guys!" Sophia Rizzo waved at us as she and Patrick Morris walked into Casey's together.

It was Sunday afternoon and we were all still pretty excited about the concert last night.

"That was really cool how Johnny Buck actually announced you guys at the concert last night," Patrick said, reaching for Sophia's hand.

"Yeah, I heard you guys had backstage passes too," Sophia chimed in. She was twirling a single red rose between her fingers.

"We sure did," I told her. I loved telling people about this. "When the concert was over, we went around back and this guy named Julio met us—"

"At first he acted really tough," Jessica interrupted. "Like he didn't believe we were really the Unicorns—"

"That's because there were other girls who claimed *they* were the Unicorns," Lila put in.

Sophia held up her hand. "I'd really like to hear all about it," she said, smiling up at Patrick. "But today is our one-year anniversary of our first date, and, well—"

"We sort of want to be alone," Patrick said apologetically.

"You understand, don't you?" Sophia asked.

"Yeah, sure," Lila and Jessica said.

"Whatever," Mandy said.

"We'll see you guys later." Patrick smiled at us. Then he turned to Sophia. "Would you like some ice cream?"

"Sure." Sophia grinned.

Patrick stepped aside and let Sophia go first. *Now that's the way a guy* should *treat a girl,* I thought.

Ellen seemed to be thinking the same thing. "Wow," she sighed, watching them wistfully. "I can't imagine anyone ever treating me like that."

I nudged her with my toe. "Don't tell me you have a crush on Patrick Morris."

Ellen blushed. "Of course not. But, well, it would be nice if once in a while *someone* would buy me some ice cream." She sighed again. "I guess I'm just not the kind of person who ever has a boyfriend."

Will Ellen find a boyfriend? Read THE UNICORN CLUB #16, **Bon Voyage, Unicorns!** *Book one in the Unicorns-at-sea two-part miniseries.*

SIGN UP FOR THE SWEET VALLEY HIGH® FAN CLUB!

Hey, girls! Get all the gossip on Sweet Valley High's® most popular teenagers when you join our fantastic Fan Club! As a member, you'll get all of this really cool stuff:

- Membership Card with your own personal Fan Club ID number
- A Sweet Valley High® Secret Treasure Box
- Sweet Valley High® Stationery
- Official Fan Club Pencil (for secret note writing!)
- Three Bookmarks
- A "Members Only" Door Hanger
- Two Skeins of J. & P. Coats® Embroidery Floss with flower barrette instruction leaflet
- Two editions of *The Oracle* newsletter
- Plus exclusive Sweet Valley High® product offers, special savings, contests, and much more!

Be the first to find out what Jessica & Elizabeth Wakefield are up to by joining the Sweet Valley High® Fan Club for the one-year membership fee of only $6.25 each for U.S. residents, $8.25 for Canadian residents (U.S. currency). Includes shipping & handling.

Send a check or money order (do not send cash) made payable to "Sweet Valley High® Fan Club" along with this form to:

SWEET VALLEY HIGH® FAN CLUB, BOX 3919-B, SCHAUMBURG, IL 60168-3919

NAME_____
(Please print clearly)

ADDRESS_____

CITY_____ STATE _____ ZIP_____
(Required)

AGE_____ BIRTHDAY_____ /_____ /_____